Dirty GAMES

A TROPICAL TEMPTATION NOVEL

Dirty GAMES

A TROPICAL TEMPTATION NOVEL

SAMANTHE BECK

This book is a work of fiction. Names, characters, places, and incidents are the product of the author's imagination or are used fictitiously. Any resemblance to actual events, locales, or persons, living or dead, is coincidental.

Entangled Publishing, LLC
2614 South Timberline Road
Suite 105, PMB 159
Fort Collins, CO 80525
Visit our website at www.entangledpublishing.com.

Brazen is an imprint of Entangled Publishing, LLC. For more information on our titles, visit www.brazenbooks.com.

Edited by Brenda Chin
Cover design by Cover Couture
Cover art from DepositPhotos

Manufactured in the United States of America

First Edition November 2017

To Brenda Freakin' Chin!

Chapter One

Quinn Sheridan found herself trapped in the taunting, neon-blue gaze of a raven-haired temptress with killer legs, a tiny waist, and improbably generous yet gravity-defiant tits challenging the limits of a painted-on black cat suit. A tremble of intimidation left tiny fractures in the bedrock of her self-assurance, but she refused to crumble. Sure, the framed poster hanging in the hall outside her agent's office presented video game vixen Lena Xavier in all her unattainably perfect, CGI-embellished glory, but with the magic of makeup, good lighting, and a little help from wardrobe, the flesh-and-blood actress hired to portray the icon of male adolescent fantasies would look the part.

Wouldn't she?

She backed up a step and caught her reflection superimposed like a pale, indistinct ghost over the image thanks to the glass protecting the lithograph. The effect wasn't particularly encouraging.

She would. Her spine straightened at the mental affirmation, and she ignored the way the woman in the poster seemed to smirk at her. Of course she would pull off the transformation. She had to.

Lifting her chin, she walked into her agent's office projecting a calm confidence she was far from feeling. The performance would have won her a standing ovation from the toughest audience. She hadn't been this anxious about a meeting since her days as an aspiring actress, about to give her first audition. But, frankly, there was a lot more at stake today.

Eddie looked up as she entered. His everglade-green eyes widened a fraction and he abandoned whatever instructions he'd been giving his assistant over his speakerphone in favor of a brusque, decisive, "Cancel lunch."

Quinn's stomach—her *empty* stomach—sank to the glossy red soles of her Louboutins.

His assistant responded first. "Eddie Washington, I sold a kidney to get you your favorite table at Toscanova. Do *not* make me call them back and cancel."

"Cancel," Eddie repeated. Quinn forced herself to stand tall and proud as his sharp gaze inspected her from the top of her upswept hair to the pointy tips of her pumps. "Cancel anything constituting a photo op for the foreseeable future, as well." He hung up on his assistant's muttered curse, pinched the bridge of his nose, and shook his head at her. "You're not camera ready."

So much for the magic of strategically gathered black jersey, and a two-hundred-dollar torture device some fashion marketing genius had the *cajones* to call a comfort-shaper. The stupid thing was *not* comfortable, and apparently, it revealed a little too much of her current shape. Which meant when it came to stupid, she won the prize.

Quinn continued into Eddie's office, swallowing the defensive excuses that leaped to her lips. She perched on the arm of the white leather divan situated against the wall opposite his desk. Excuses wouldn't change anything. Nor would getting defensive. Acting wasn't a career for fragile egos, and she didn't pay him to coddle hers.

They'd known each other a long time—since those early days when her twin brother, Callum, had been the real client and she'd been a little extra baggage their mother had negotiated into the deal. Eddie was one of the top sports and entertainment agents, as well as one of her oldest friends, and she was lucky to have him. While his brutal honesty stung, he had her best interests at heart. *Their* best interests.

Keeping that in mind, she folded her arms across her more ample than normal chest, lifted one brow, and shot him her trademark half smile—the cool facade that gave nothing away. "Okay, fine. I've let my conditioning slip a little."

"A *little*?" He got up and strode around his glass monument of a desk. The thick, white rug hushed his footsteps.

Inside, she winced. Outwardly, she just shrugged. "I took a couple weeks off after *Pep Rally* wrapped. I'd earned a break."

Propping his enviably toned frame against his desk, he inspected her again. "Absolutely. But this"—he gestured at her—"is not the result of taking a break for 'a couple weeks.'" Restless fingers formed air quotes around the words. "You've lost all the lean muscle and definition the studio expects for this kind of a role. You were supposed to spend the hiatus turning yourself from a cheerleader into a big-screen, action heroine. If they get a look at you now, they're going to think you're undisciplined or indifferent about the role. We both know you're neither." His eyes narrowed with something suspiciously like concern. "What happened?"

"Nothing." She scoffed the word, but her conscience cringed. Her twin brother had happened. A busted knee had happened. Eight weeks of sitting around nursing the sprain with a steady diet of regret and carbs had happened. And yes, apparently all the inactivity had taken a toll. Her bathroom scale hadn't actually moved all that much, but her clothes fit differently. Her favorite shirts felt snugger across the chest. Her favorite jeans hugged tighter to her hips. Her stomach wasn't quite as taut and flat as it had been before the injury. She still couldn't quite believe it. Between years of acting classes, dance lessons, rehearsals, and a good metabolism, she'd always been able to maintain her shape without giving it any concentrated effort.

Eddie continued to regard her, but now doubt drove his eyebrows toward his hairline. "Nothing happened?" he asked again.

"I took a break. That's all. And fine, maybe I let myself go a bit." She shrugged and examined her cuticles as if a hangnail worried her more than this conversation. "It's not a big deal."

"Not if your next job involved posing for *Playboy*." Eddie raked a hand through his short afro, making his dark hair stand on end. "But double-agent, martial arts master, and all-around ass kicker Lena Xavier is supposed to look dangerously sexy. The producers want Wonder Woman, Lara Croft, and Atomic Blonde all rolled into one, and zipped into a skintight leather cat suit. Instead you're bombshell curvy, and…wait. You're not pregnant, are you?"

A harsh laugh slipped out. "Ha. Right. Alert the media. Call the Pope. We've got another immaculate conception." The last six months had been hell on her social life. There were reasons. Several, actually—the sprained knee being perhaps the least of them—but though Eddie held a position of trust in her life, she didn't intend to share any of them with him.

He let out what might have been a sigh of relief, but shook his head. "We're not calling anyone. If the studio brass get a load of you looking like this…" He let the implications go unstated and combed his fingers through his hair again. "Hell, I'm pretty sure there's an appearance clause in your contract, which means—"

"I know what it means." The producers could fire her at any time during filming if her appearance changed even slightly from the way she'd looked at the time she'd been cast in the role. Of course they could. Audiences expected their favorite anti-hero spy to make the leap from Xbox to big screen while wearing her iconic cat suit. The actress playing her had to do the role justice.

And she *would*. But "during filming" seemed like the operative phrase here. Filming didn't start for three months. A comforting thought, but the flickers of panic in Eddie's eyes put a skip in her pulse. She stood, moved to the center of the sofa, and took a proper seat this time. "Is that what this meeting is all about? You want to make sure I'll be camera ready? Relax." She ran her palms over the length of her dress. "Twelve weeks is plenty of time to tighten the assets, so there's no need to body shame me into—"

"Six weeks."

She jerked her attention back to Eddie. "What?"

"They moved up the shooting schedule because of a change in the location availability. You're due in wardrobe in just over six weeks. *That's* why I called this meeting."

"Oh…fuck me. You're kidding."

He pulled his handsome face into a grimace. "I don't kid about business."

Fuck, indeed. After spending the last five years singing, dancing, and acting her ass off as the perky head cheerleader on the hit television series *Pep Rally*—and turning down film after film because Hollywood wanted to typecast her as a bouncy blonde—fate had rewarded her patience with a starring role in *Dirty Games*, the big-budget film based on the best-selling video game. It had taken half a decade, but she'd finally graduated from high school. This was a major move for her, the chance to transition from the small screen to the big one, from teen starlet to bankable box office draw. She wanted this shot. She needed it, personally and financially. And she'd damn well earned it. But plenty of people would love to see her fail. Especially any of the actresses who'd made the short list to play Lena. This was a competitive industry.

Sunlight streamed through the floor-to-ceiling windows along one wall of the office, slanted across the sofa, and created an uncomfortably hot spotlight directly where she sat. "Okay. Don't give yourself an aneurysm. I've got this under control. I'll get in shape."

He stared at her for a long moment while he turned something over in his mind. "Six weeks leaves no margin for error. I'm calling in professional help."

Professional help? "You're referring me to a therapist?"

"Sort of. I'm sure he'll fix whatever's going on in your head at the same time he fixes the rest of you." Then he strode behind his desk and spoke into his phone. "Lisa, get the secret weapon on this line, ASAP." His gaze slid to her. "Tell him it's an emergency." Without waiting for a reply, he disconnected, and flung himself into his chair. Over steepled fingers, he looked at Quinn.

Something in his stare sent a trickle of sweat down her spine. "What's the 'secret weapon'?"

A beat of silence followed her question, broken by the squeak of Eddie's leather chair as he leaned forward. "Luke McLean. He spent over a decade as a private fitness consultant to the biggest names in Hollywood. Over the last couple years, he's changed his focus somewhat, but he'll take you on as a favor to me, if I ask him. He's exclusive, and expensive, but he always gets results."

An expensive workout buddy? No thanks. "That's sweet of you to offer, but I can do this myself."

"You've never dieted or hit the gym in your life," Eddie argued.

"If you don't think rehearsing and performing the *Pep Rally* routines counts as working out, I'd like to see you do it."

"I'm sure it was, but you don't have that now. What you have is six weeks to get yourself back into the kind of shape you took for granted when you were eighteen, except, hey, you're not eighteen anymore." He shook his head slowly.

She had a feeling he wasn't sure if even his secret weapon could pull this off. "Thanks for pointing that out," she retorted, unable to keep the snap of sarcasm at bay.

"Look, things change as you age—"

"I'm twenty-three!"

"Right. You're not a teenager. This is going to take effort, and a plan."

"Eddie, I have a plan. Eat less. Move more." It wasn't rocket science, for God's sake. Besides, the change in her physique had nothing to do with her age, and everything to do with weeks of limited activity resulting from the sprained MCL she'd incurred while literally dragging Callum to a long-overdue stint at a private rehab facility.

Thankfully, she hadn't needed surgery to repair the ligament. A clunky brace and six weeks of PT had done the trick. Now that her doctor had given her a clean bill of health, she could spend some quality time in the small home gym she'd installed—the one Callum had used maybe a handful of times before sliding back into the old habits their mom had been naive enough to think Quinn could save him from.

Mom had been wrong, as it turned out. She was nobody's savior, despite her mother's insistence on casting her in the role of dependable, responsible twin. No matter how hard she tried, and how much she missed the old Callum, she couldn't solve his problems for him. But she *could* solve her own. Hop on the treadmill or elliptical every morning for thirty minutes or so, and turn herself into Lena Xavier. How hard could it be? She didn't need some overpriced expert telling her what to do.

"Talk to me about negative calories," Eddie challenged. "Describe an optimal cardio-strength training balance for burning fat and building lean muscle."

"Just because I don't speak *Muscle & Fitness*, doesn't mean I don't know how to—"

Eddie's phone buzzed. He held up a finger to silence her, and spoke into the speaker. "Give me good news, Lisa."

"I've got Mr. McLean on the line."

"Put him through, and take an extra half hour for lunch."

"I'm taking an extra hour. Seems I scored a prime table at Toscanova. Since it's going on your Amex, I'll bring you a panini. Line one."

Eddie rolled his eyes, and tapped the line. "Luke, my man. Thanks for getting in touch so quickly."

"Your assistant said it was an emergency."

The deep, slightly impatient response vibrated with an edge of authority that did funny things to her insides—the kind of things that had her recrossing her legs and pressing her thighs together. She had a little weakness for growly voices. And authority.

"It is," Eddie said. "I need you to take on a full-time client, for the next six weeks—"

"Impossible."

"Nothing's impossible."

"This is. I don't take on private clients anymore. Even if I did, I can't do this one. I'm leaving at the end of the week for my first real vacation in three years. I can refer you to a couple of qualified consultants who might be able to help."

"I don't need a referral. I need you. You're the best."

A cynical laugh sent something hot and restless fluttering low in Quinn's abdomen. "Kissing ass won't change anything."

"I'm just stating a fact," Eddie replied smoothly. "Want to know another fact? Everything's negotiable. What will it take to make this happen? Name your price. Name the place. My only requirement is that it be absolutely private and totally confidential."

"You can't put a price on mental health. I need a vacation. For the past three years I've been one hundred percent focused on building my business. The facility, the staff, and the referral network—"

"Mortgage, insurance, salaries…all this requires cash, does it not?"

"I'm comfortable with my burn rate," the low voice replied, with a calm that backed up the confidence of the statement. "Call Rick Samson, or Julianna Pierce."

"He's a glorified rep counter, and she's insane. Come on, Luke. Remember having an hour of need? This is mine."

A long silence followed. Quinn found herself holding her breath. Half of her hoped he'd refuse. No, correction, *all* of her hoped he'd refuse. She didn't want to put herself in the hands of some arrogant stranger who clearly didn't want the gig.

"Dammit, Eddie."

Those clipped words came out lower. Harsher. The little hairs on her arm stood at attention.

"Sorry, man. I wouldn't play the 'you owe me' card if this wasn't important. I'm at your mercy."

Her imagination cracked under the pressure, and sought its own escape by conjuring up an image of her strapped to some complicated piece of gym equipment, her muscles straining and immobilized, and that gruff voice telling her she was at *his* mercy.

A frustrated groan came from the other end of the line. Her hard-up hormones created an entirely different scenario for the thigh-tightening sound. He followed it up with a reluctant, "What's the goal?"

Eddie pumped a fist in victory. "You'll do it?"

"I'm not committing to anything, yet. First, I have to understand what *it* is, and if I think I can get *it* done. Then, you still have to agree to my terms."

"My client needs to get chiseled like a slab of granite. No bulking, just cut, cut, cut. Define and tone"—Eddie glanced her way again—"everything, in six weeks."

"Cut, define, and tone in six weeks? Your client's aggressive."

"That's why I need you. You specialize in aggressive."

The phone's speaker carried the sound of a long, forceful exhale. Her cheeks heated at the humiliation of being discussed like an unappealing project, but at the same time, her lips tingled as if the gust of air he'd released from deep in his chest had breezed over them. Pathetic or not, this phone call was the most action she'd gotten in…forever.

"Age? Injuries? I have to assume there's a reason an athlete with the talent to warrant your representation has let his training lapse."

"Twenty-three, no injuries, and she's not an athlete. Her name is Quinn Sheridan, and she's preparing for a movie role—"

"Oh *hell* no, Eddie." The voice now held an indignant note. "Not an actress. Anything but an actress."

Heat burned her face for a whole different reason. Anger. How dare this self-righteous jackass reject her, based on her career choice?

Eddie sent her a sharp look, held up a hand, and closed it like a mouth to send her the universal sign for "shut it." "My hour of need," he reiterated into the speaker.

"Fine." The brusque word practically slapped her. "But this is way more than an hour of need, and my time comes at a cost." Then he proceeded to name a figure that stole her breath. Before she could find her voice and utter a flat-out rejection, he added, "Plus expenses."

"Done," Eddie said. "Half up front, and half at the end, provided she's camera-ready from every angle by the time you're finished with her. Where do you want to do this?"

"The Playground at Paradise Bay," he responded, naming one of the priciest, most exclusive destinations in the Caribbean. "I've used them in the past for this type of thing, so I know the resort offers everything we need, including unparalleled privacy. They have excellent facilities, their chefs can accommodate my customized menus, and I can keep your client focused on her goal in such a contained environment."

Holy crap. A hefty chunk of her Lena Xavier paycheck was disappearing before her eyes, and she hadn't earned a penny of it yet. But she needed to, because private drug treatment facilities like Foundations carried a hefty price tag, and thanks to some bad financial decisions on her parents' part, they weren't in a position to help cover the cost of Callum's rehab. It was all on her. Every penny.

"Reserve one of the villas," McLean went on, squandering even more of her money without hesitation. "One with a workout room included."

"My assistant will send you the reservation confirmation and your flight information by the end of the day," Eddie replied. "Anything else?"

She lowered her forehead to her knees and waited for a lightheaded feeling to pass.

"Yeah. Convey this to your client…"

The note of steel in the words had her straightening, and staring at the phone.

"I have a zero bullshit policy," he went on. "I won't tolerate diva behavior from some neurotic, narcissistic actress who expects everyone to cater to her bottomless ego. Tell her to leave the entourage at home. I'm taking *her* on, not her boyfriend, her girlfriend, her mother, or her spiritual advisor. For six weeks, I'm in charge. I expect her to obey instructions and adhere to the program. No exceptions, no excuses, or no deal."

"Uh..." Eddie had the grace to wince. "Did you get that, Quinn?"

She hauled herself to her feet—toned or not, she could damn well stand up for herself—and strode to his desk until she was close enough to brace her palms on the cool glass, and leaned toward the phone. "Every word," she said in her best ice-bitch voice. "Luckily, neither my neurosis nor my narcissism interferes with my hearing. Tell Mr. McLean I'll see him in Paradise Bay."

Chapter Two

Luke McLean stepped onto the patio of the Paradise Bar—The Playground's version of casual lounging—and scanned the tanned bodies in beachwear soaking in some final rays of sunlight before the first drinks of the evening. This was his one night to himself before he spent six weeks whipping a spoiled starlet into shape, and he planned to enjoy it.

A group of women in tiny bikinis walked by, enveloping him in the scent of coconut, and the pull of lingering gazes. Yeah, he'd definitely enjoy tonight. But despite the generous display of sun-kissed skin all around him, nobody really caught his eye, except… His attention snagged on a woman perched on one of the stools at the bar, chatting with the bartender. She sat in profile to him, but even in this sea of beauty, she stood out.

It wasn't the waves of Scandinavian-blond hair tumbling to her shoulders, or wide-set eyes lit with a seductive sparkle. No, he corrected as she tipped her head to the side, and those eyes strayed his way. Challenge. They sparked with challenge. And while he appreciated a good challenge more than most, the inherent provocation wasn't what captured his attention. It also wasn't the cock-teasing curves set off to perfection by a miniscule white bikini—though plenty of other guys on the terrace noticed them.

It was her mouth that enslaved him. A soft, pink cupid bow perpetually turned up at one corner in a wicked little smile. A hint that suggested this angel had a devilish side, and the irony of it amused the hell out of her.

While he watched, she took a sip of her drink. Her throat worked as she swallowed, and then her tongue took a leisurely pass along her damp lips. First the top, then the bottom. By the time her mouth settled into the Mona Lisa smile again, his balls throbbed hard enough to make him curse under his breath. He wanted to see her swallow and lick her lips like that again—just like that—after he jacked himself off in her sinful mouth. Oblivious to the havoc she wreaked mere feet away, she batted her eyes at the bartender, and laughed at something he said.

That laugh. Low. Throaty. Completely uncensored and obscenely sexy. Around the bar, heads turned, and a bunch of Wall Street ballers in board shorts and brand new tans wondered in silent unison if she made an equally sultry sound when she came. A totally unwarranted, but shockingly strong surge of possessiveness raged through him. Anthropologists might label it a primitive remnant from a time when the appropriate response to competition for the most desirable female involved thumping his chest, roaring, and intimidating all others away with a show of strength and dominance. Then he'd claim his prize, right there in the sand, with her blond hair roped around his fist and his balls slapping her ass until the lush curves turned the same ripe pink as her lips. He imagined thrusting, and thrusting, and thrusting, so his lungs burned and his muscles screamed. Until she reared up, her body clenching and quivering around him, and cried out in gratitude, using that same husky voice.

The larger, more evolved part of his brain pointed out that if this beautiful stranger had the faintest idea what kind of rogue Neanderthal impulses had hijacked his thoughts, she'd slap *him* so fast his head would spin. If not literally slap him, then hit him with a restraining order. Possibly both.

Or maybe not. As if equally primitive receptors somewhere inside her picked up on the testosterone blasting off him like heat from a furnace, she turned and looked straight at him, and…

Damn.

Reality was what slapped him, hard, leaving behind a cold sting of frustration that did nothing to burn away the lust.

Quinn Sheridan. According to Eddie, she wasn't supposed to arrive until tomorrow morning. Apparently, she'd caught an earlier flight.

No two-dimensional medium did her justice. The woman sitting ten feet away at the bar looked like exactly that—a woman—rather than the kittenish cheerleader he'd watched sing, dance, and connive her way through the screener Eddie had sent him so he could see what his new client 'should' look like.

Personally, he begged to differ. Her current BMI put her at the curvaceous end of the healthy spectrum, and squarely into male fantasy territory—his, at any rate—but professionally, he understood Eddie's concern. The movie role she'd signed on for required she look sleek and nimble as a lynx. Someone not to be fucked with. Right now she looked entirely too…fuckable. Want sliced through him. Hot and sharp, and not her fault, despite how easy it would be to lay the blame at her feet.

Note to self. You don't fuck actresses. No, he did not. Not anymore. He'd done his share during his ten years in

Hollywood, and he refused to reboard that particular crazy-train. He also didn't fuck clients. And he absolutely, positively did not fuck actresses who were clients.

Her attention lingered on him this time, so undisguised he thought for a moment she realized who he was, and was about to say something to him. Maybe he hadn't been the only one to do some research before arriving?

The gaze wandered lower, moving over him as slowly and thoroughly as an appraisal. By the time she finished looking her fill, his whole body ached. Then the little tease picked up a spoon, dug into a confection of whipped cream and chocolate he hadn't noticed on a small plate in front of her, and brought it to her mouth. The spoon dripped with melted fudge and empty calories. Her lips closed around the bite, and her eyelids fluttered. She savored the mouthful for a drawn-out moment, then swallowed and licked chocolate from her lower lip. The bartender brought her another glass filled with a generous pour of something chilled and bubbly.

Lust and frustration simmered into anger. Was she really sitting there, eating chocolate and chugging champagne in front of the man her agent had emotionally extorted into helping her? Dammit, he'd put carefully laid plans aside to come here and tackle this "emergency." And she wasn't taking it seriously. Granted, their six weeks didn't start until tomorrow at noon, and maybe she didn't actually realize who he was, but this sneak peek at her commitment level didn't impress him.

Time to lay down the law.

She straightened as he approached, and aimed the sly smile at him, but no flicker of recognition crossed her features. She didn't know who he was. At least there was that. She hadn't deliberately flaunted her bad behavior at him, but even so, she'd definitely earned a warning.

He stepped into the empty space between her chair and

one occupied by the female half of a very affectionate couple sharing an oversize umbrella drink. Restoring the Texas drawl fifteen years in Los Angeles had eroded, he led with a relaxed, "Sorry for staring, but aren't you—"

"No." She let the smile turn apologetic and lowered her eyelids. "I get that a lot, but no, I'm not her." Long, naked eyelashes flicked up to reveal guileless eyes as clear and blue as the Caribbean shimmering in the distance. "I hope you're not too disappointed?"

He had to hand it to her. She had this act down pat. "Somehow, I doubt you've ever disappointed." Leaning a forearm on the bar, he eased closer. "Now that I see you up close, I realize you're much prettier than what's-her-face."

"Quinn Sheridan?" She couldn't quite hide the hint of irritation in her voice at the backhanded compliment.

"I guess that's her name. She's got, well, you know..." He smiled vaguely, and deliberately refrained from elaborating. Knowing actors—and he did—she wouldn't be able to resist finding out what imperfection he perceived.

Her brows drew together for one fleeting moment, before she arranged her features into a show of mild curiosity. "What?"

"The plastic look. Inexpressive. Like she's had too much Botox. I guess that's what happens when a thirty-something actress plays the part of a high school student. She's got to be getting desperate to move on. She's not going to be able to pull it off much longer."

Her mouth dropped open. Inexpressive? Uh-uh. She might have a certain look she presented to the world, but her real emotions were right there beneath the surface, ready to break through. Finally, she took a long gulp of her drink before swallowing and clearing her throat.

"I'm *sure* she's not thirty-something. She looks very natural to me. I don't have a hard time buying her in the role."

He shrugged. "I guess you suspend your sense of disbelief more easily. Or, I don't know, maybe it's not her looks that throw me. Maybe it's her performance."

Color flooded her cheeks. She swiveled so that she faced him, and folded her arms over her chest. "What's wrong with her performance?"

"She comes across kind of wooden, don't you think?"

Her mouth dropped open again. She actually sputtered. "Wooden? Hell, no. She's won awards for her performance. She's been nominated for an Emmy."

He shrugged again. He'd read her bio. He knew about her Emmy noms. "Has she?"

"Twice!" Her palm slapped the bar for emphasis.

"Didn't win, though, huh?" Before she could respond, he continued, "If she's so talented, why hasn't she broken out? Could be I missed it, but I haven't seen her in anything except that show." He caught the bartender's eye. "I'll have a glass of what she's having, and—" He glanced at her. "Would you like another?"

"Yes. Thank you," she said, and under her breath added, "Bring the bottle." When the bartender moved away, she drew herself up to full height. Five feet, four inches of slightly inebriated, very pissed off actress ready to defend herself. "Maybe she was waiting for the right role? I heard she's going to be in the movie version of *Dirty Games*, and"—her white-knuckled grip on the bar offered him a small sign of her nervousness about that situation—"I think she's going to make an amazing Lena Xavier."

Now that he'd gotten her all primed to do battle, it was time to lull her into thinking she'd won. He held up his hands. "Hey, listen, I don't mean to offend you. You're obviously a fan."

Her grip on the bar relaxed a fraction. "And you're obviously not."

"My only point is, you're much prettier. *You* should be an actress. Or a model."

The compliment distracted her, and earned him a surprisingly sincere smile, but then she tossed her hair over her shoulders and sighed. "I'm too short to model, and, at the moment"—she grimaced and finished her drink—"I'm also out of shape." A busboy interrupted the unguarded moment to clear her empty glass.

"There's nothing wrong with your shape." He said it because it was the kind of response a man hitting on a woman should offer, but also because it was a fact. Anywhere except Hollywood, she'd be considered perfect, which provided yet another example of what a screwed up place Hollywood was and why he'd opted out.

The sincere smile made an encore appearance. "That's nice of you to say, but my mirror says different. I'm a dancer, but I got a little derailed a couple months ago and had to take a break. Now, I need to get back to work. So"—she fiddled with the stem of her glass— "I'm banished to Paradise for some austerity measures."

"Lucky me." He glanced pointedly at the tequila-sunset sky blazing above the horizon, and added, "And lucky you. There are worse places to be banished."

"Maybe, but tonight is probably my only chance to enjoy it." Her gaze landed meaningfully on him, full of invitation, but her fingers moved from the wineglass to her cocktail napkin, and picked at a corner. "Starting tomorrow, I'm stuck spending the next six weeks with some overpriced personal trainer my agent insisted on."

Oh yeah. They'd be adjusting her attitude. "A good trainer delivers results quickly and safely. A lot of people would say that's worth every penny."

She waved a hand as if swatting a fly. "I don't need some arrogant fitness nazi barking at me to drop and give him twenty. I'll bet this guy builds freakishly large muscles to compensate for the fact that he has a single-digit IQ, and the world's smallest dick."

The bartender chose that moment to deliver their drinks. Luke made the "check please" sign as his unsuspecting client leaned in so her breasts nearly touched his chest. The heat of her body penetrated his shirt. "Thank you for the drink. Enough about me. What brings you to Paradise Bay?"

He leaned in, too, bringing their faces close. "Work."

"What kind of work?" Her attention drifted to his mouth, then back up to look him in the eye. The blue of her irises deepened to violet around the pupils, making them seem even wider. Genetics had smiled on Quinn Sheridan, right down to the fine details. She scraped her teeth over her lower lip. His teeth itched to do the same. Itched to rough up that plush velvety flesh before he soothed it with his tongue.

The cocktail of frustration and desire she stirred in him left a bittersweet taste in his mouth. Seems they were both due for a reality check. He took her chin, absently appreciating how the faint dimple accommodated his thumb, and dropped the drawl as he answered, "I'm surprised you can't guess by my arrogance and freakishly large muscles."

Confusion clouded her eyes for a split second before realization seeped in. She tried to pull away, but he held onto her chin and kept her close. Her tongue darted out again, quickly this time, like a criminal making a prison break—and then she offered him an imperious smile. "Well played, Mr. McLean, but I knew it was you the whole time."

"Sorry, Miss Sheridan, but you're not that good an actress."

Her eyes chilled to glaciers. "Is this your version of an audition? One I failed? Am I in trouble now?"

"You *are* trouble." He released her chin. "And we're not here to play games. I'll let tonight slide, since we're not on the clock yet, but lie to me again and our deal is off." With that warning hanging in the air, he clinked his glass to hers, took a sip, and placed it on the bar. "We start tomorrow morning at nine sharp in the gym at your villa. Don't keep me waiting."

He turned and took a step away before tossing over his shoulder, "And for the record, both my IQ and my dick are well above average."

Chapter Three

Quinn pulled her hair into a ponytail as she lurched down the stairs of her villa and tried to ignore the pounding at the back of her skull. Retina-scorching sunbeams poured through tall patio doors and bounced off the white walls. Squinting, she fumbled her way into the open kitchen with its gleaming granite countertops and grabbed her sunglasses from where she'd tossed them yesterday evening after returning from the debacle of her first meeting with Luke McLean.

Oh God, the fourth glass of champagne had been a mistake. Truth. She wasn't much of a drinker, but she'd given in to a rare bout of loneliness and self-pity yesterday evening, and alcohol had been her only sympathetic friend. Later, it had helped ease the sting of getting setup and knocked down like a bowling pin by the one man on this entire island with whom she'd intended to establish the upper hand.

She shoved the sunglasses on and faced the reality she'd used her buddy Dom to hide from last night. *McLean won round one. You lost. Shake it off.*

Good advice. Too bad she couldn't get her ego to play

along. The judgmental bastard had insulted her before he'd even clapped eyes on her, with his superior attitude and knee-jerk disdain for her profession, her situation, and, well, basically everything about her. Worse than the self-defensive anger he'd pulled out of her was the hurt. He'd hurt her feelings, dammit, and few people had the power to do that—certainly not strangers.

She was no special snowflake. Growing up in the business had toughened her soul. During her early years, she'd dealt with the frustration of sitting in Callum's shadow, all but invisible, watching him garner praise and attention as his career soared and hers stalled on the runway. Even now, as an established actress in her own right, she handled skepticism, criticism, and plain old rejection on a regular basis, and she did it without crying on anyone's shoulder. But Luke? For whatever reason, she couldn't handle him. His low opinion hit some vulnerable crevice inside her where insecurity rooted, despite all her attempts to pave it over.

Why?

Answering that question forced her to face the most uncomfortable fact of all. She took a bottle of water from the fridge, and then paused there to let the cool air—and the sad truth—flow over her hot face. She was attracted to the man. From the second she'd heard his disembodied voice over Eddie's phone, some purely feminine and neglected parts had roused and taken notice. But Luke McLean embodied, absolutely captivated them. They responded to more than sun-burnished brown hair her fingers wanted to comb through, or the tall, masculine frame reinforced with honed muscle as naturally breathtaking and imposing as a sequoia. In her business, she routinely encountered sculpted jaws and zero percent body fat. It took more than that to turn her head. But damn him, he had more.

Even in something as innocuous as a T-shirt and shorts,

strength and confidence flowed from every pore, and yes, she would have loved to crash up against that athletic body, feel it jar hers as lean hips and hard thighs pumped pleasure into her with every thrust.

You're going to have to climb into the freezer if you keep this up.

Right. She shut the fridge and then turned to search for Advil in the basket of goodies hospitality had left on the kitchen island. This is where inadvertently banishing herself to a sexual desert for half a year got her—so pent-up, a well-packaged set of XY chromosomes could throw her off her game.

Not entirely, she acknowledged as she tore open a small packet and swallowed the blue gelcaps. She couldn't blame her response to him solely on the physical promise inherent in such an awe-inspiring example of the male species, because the part of him that really got under her skin was his…intensity. When his steady hazel gaze inspected her, it took measure on every level, as if he saw past the normal distractions most people got caught up in—blond hair, nice rack, a quick, sardonic smile—and looked straight into *her.* They judged. Hell yes, they did, but not strictly on appearance in the way she'd grown accustomed to encountering. And maybe because she wasn't accustomed to anyone looking deeper, his assessment stripped her of her standard defenses. She found herself searching those inscrutable depths for…it killed her to admit it…some sign of approval. Like a freaking kindergartner standing before her teacher, reciting the alphabet.

She hadn't found it, at least not last night. She'd seen male admiration. He'd given her that much—and she recognized it well enough to know it hadn't been part of his act—but he'd withheld approval. More aptly, he'd woven it into a red flag of sexual chemistry and waved it in her face. Then boom. She'd charged headlong into a brick wall of rejection.

Her skull pounded in agreement. To be fair, maybe she'd had it coming. No fitness consultant worth his fee would pat a client on the back for selecting champagne and molten chocolate cake for dinner. But last night, she'd still been on her time, not his, and was it really so weak to enjoy one final indulgence before submitting to six weeks of some unholy regimen?

Um…you also called him an arrogant fitness nazi with freakishly large muscles, a single-digit IQ, and the world's smallest dick.

The memory pried a laugh out of her—one she immediately paid for when her headache flared. She bit her lip and inhaled a cautious breath through her nose. He'd had *that* coming, for being such a jerk when Eddie had called. Unwittingly insulting him to his face hardly qualified as her finest moment, but…whatever. He'd pigeonholed her as a narcissistic, neurotic actress, and nothing she did now was likely to change his closed little mind. She considered him an arrogant ass, because he was. Ultimately, it didn't matter what they thought of each other. She was the client, and she was paying him—exorbitantly—to do a job. He could keep his personal opinions to himself. She toasted that with a swallow of water.

Her stomach rumbled, and she thought briefly about grabbing an energy bar from the goody basket, but with only a minute until nine, she didn't have time. God forbid she arrive a second late for her first morning of supervised torture. Luke McLean would walk—which didn't necessarily worry her—but then Eddie would murder her. And that would be a problem.

Contenting herself with another sip of water, she wound her way to the wall of soaring plantation shutters someone had been nice enough to open in preparation for her arrival.

She stepped out onto the cobblestone patio surrounded by tall palms, curling ferns, and privacy walls covered in flowering vines. The scent of jasmine-infused air was so heavy, it made her want to stretch out on one of the lounge chairs surrounding the pool and do nothing more strenuous than watch paper-thin purple bougainvillea blossoms float across the glassy surface of the water. Instead she marched past the chairs to the smaller building on the opposite side of the courtyard. The little pool house looked like a charming bungalow, with its covered porch cooled by the lazy rotations of two woven rattan ceiling fans. But looks could be deceiving. She knew this from the self-guided tour she'd braved last night. Beyond the rustic slatted doors lay a room full of equipment and mirrors that promised to be her personal torture chamber for the next six weeks.

The doors opened as she approached, and there he was—her oppressor—in all his scowling, stone-jawed glory. Flinty eyes inspected her from her on-the-fly ponytail to the laces of her Puma Pulses.

"Right on time, Trouble. Come in, strip down, and we'll get started."

• • •

Dark blond brows arched over the reflective lenses of polarized aviators. "Maybe you should call a woman by her actual name before you tell her to strip?"

He'd expected a smart-ass reply. Not because he'd instructed her to remove her clothes—the modesty quotient tended to be pretty low with the actors and athletes he'd worked with—but because he'd instructed her at all. She didn't think she needed him. She sure as hell didn't respect his expertise, and she didn't care to listen to anything he had to say. True respect had to be earned, but by the end of this session, she'd know she needed him. That would be lesson number one.

He shut the doors behind her, then turned to face her and crossed his arms. Many clients found it an intimidating experience, staring down six foot, three inches and 230 pounds of external motivation, but this one was an exception. She stood there in her slouchy gray-and-black zip-front hoodie and matching jogger pants, nearly a foot shorter than him and over a hundred pounds lighter, and deliberately took a long, slow drink from her water bottle before crossing her arms to mimic his pose.

"Maybe you should read the information my client coordinator sent you concerning proper workout attire, Quinn. But since you obviously didn't, strip down to your underwear, and stand over there." He pointed to one end of the workout room where a sand-colored wall formed a neutral background. "We'll start with a photo session."

And an assessment, but that was mainly for him. The photos were mainly for her. He didn't airbrush, or aim for the most flattering angle. Despite how much time they spent in front of a camera, a surprising percentage of his industry clients found the straight, unfiltered truth eye-opening.

Her little, dimpled chin came up a notch. "I dance in clothes like these all the time." She tossed her empty water bottle into the bin beside the door. "What's wrong with what I'm wearing, Mr. McLean?"

"Luke," he corrected, and slid the sunglasses off her face.

"Hey..." She blinked, and took an automatic step back, nearly falling over a workout bench before he wrapped a hand around her upper arm and caught her. "This place is a death trap," she muttered, and then shot him a glare when he didn't release her.

"It can be. Which is why we have rules."

"Rules...right. I remember your rules from our lovely

conversation in Eddie's office. Keep my neurosis and narcissism under control and don't expect you to cater to my whims. I think that sums it up." Her eyes went wide and innocent. "Gosh. I don't remember the part where I agreed to let you dictate what I wear."

Her voice could freeze a man's balls off, but her expression revealed traces of weariness he felt sure she didn't realize she showed. He stifled a sigh, released her arm, and hung her sunglasses from the neck of his T-shirt. Yes, her attitude sucked, but part of the reason was because of him. They'd gotten off on the wrong foot, thanks to Eddie's call—and his uncensored reaction to discovering his friend had coerced him into precisely the kind of job he'd sworn off. He'd founded McLean Fitness to help regular people overcome weight management challenges, and make real, lasting changes in their lives. Catering to overprivileged, appearance-obsessed clients no longer fulfilled him.

Still, none of that was her doing. The neurotic, narcissistic bit had been a generalization meant to convey to Eddie how frustrated he was with the whole request. It hadn't been directed at Quinn personally, and it certainly hadn't been intended for her ears. But, of course, she *had* taken it personally, and immediately labeled him an adversary. Normally, he didn't give a shit what label he wore, as long as he got results. And adversarial relationships could produce dramatic results, as any drill sergeant would attest, but not if it meant she fought him every step of the way.

And she was definitely fighting him. Every. Damn. Step.

Those tired, distrustful eyes only confirmed that... as well as the fact that this morning she was paying for her champagne binge last night. She needed some decent nourishment, at least one more bottle of water, and a couple additional hours of sleep. Aside from the water, she'd have to get the others on her own time. But he could give her an explanation, if for no other reason than to demonstrate he wasn't being an arbitrary wardrobe dictator.

"There are several problems with what you're wearing." He turned her around and marched her through a jungle of Precor machines until they stood facing one of the mirrored walls. "First, loose clothes are a hazard in the gym. They can get snagged on equipment"—he tugged on the pocket of her hoodie hard enough to pull her off-balance, and then took hold of her shoulders and righted her—"or caught in the moving parts. In either case, you end up injured. I refuse to let that happen. Next, we both need to be able to see your body during workouts." He unzipped the hoodie and drew it down her arms, revealing a small black sports bra that showed off all the generous cleavage he remembered from yesterday evening at the hotel bar, and from the dreams he'd tossed, and turned, and groaned his way through last night.

"Like what you see?"

Everything about her provoked—the question, her arched brows, and the hint of a smile curving her lips. He ignored all of it. Most of him did, at any rate, because rising to the provocation went against every professional and personal ethic he possessed. But it shouldn't have been so painfully difficult, goddammit. He'd worked with many spectacularly beautiful women over the years. Quinn Sheridan was just another one in a long list. A client. End of story. Luckily, her body blocked a view of the part of him finding the limits of their situation hardest to ignore.

To buy another moment, he draped her jacket over a rack of free weights, and then turned to face her in the mirror again. "I like being able to see if you're doing the moves properly, so I can correct you if necessary."

"And this requires me to run around in next to nothing?" Her gaze narrowed. "Give you a free show over the next six weeks? That's a nice bonus for you." She turned to face him, and dialed the smile up a notch. "What bonus do *I* get out of it?"

Okay, they needed to clarify this right here, right now. "Over the next six weeks I'm going to see and handle damn near every inch of you, but that's not a bonus for either of us. That's me doing my job. I'm your medic, chiropractor, and physical therapist all rolled into one. Before we're done, I'll also be your shrink, your coach, your cheerleader, and your taskmaster, but what I will not be, Quinn, is your fuck toy. That is not part of the services you're paying me to perform. Are we clear?"

Her face paled, save for two slashes of crimson across each stunning cheekbone, which couldn't have been starker if he'd actually slapped her. "Crystal," she managed, and then turned her back on him and started toeing off her shoes.

Shit. He'd pounded that point home more brutally than necessary—mostly in an effort to get the message through his own thick skull—but she'd been on the receiving end of his frustration. She'd simply been taunting him, and testing him, because there was a big, horny elephant in the room and neither of them could pretend it wasn't there. In an attempt to make it go away, he'd ended up insulting them both.

With her back still to him, she bent over and peeled her pants off, leaving her in snug, black shorts-style panties. Really snug. Really short. The fabric stretched low across her hips but ended high enough to leave plenty of territory bare. The bikini she'd worn yesterday had been smaller and more revealing, but he still had to close his eyes for a moment to block out the sight of her heart-shaped ass packaged up like a gift not quite contained by the wrapper. Sweat-drenched nocturnal fantasies from last night resurfaced—fisted sheets, tangled limbs, thighs parted wide and that ass lifted high while her sultry voice echoed in his mind. *Yes, Luke. Yes to anything. Everything. All you want. Yes.*

Christ. This favor to Eddie was going to be the end of him. He ground his teeth and opened his eyes. She straightened, and their gazes clashed in the mirror.

"Just for the record, Luke, I don't have to pay men to sleep with me."

Chapter Four

The son of a bitch had the decency to look away first. He stared a hole through the wall while a muscle ticked in his jaw, and a flush of color rose in his cheeks, though whether anger, embarrassment, or exasperation brought about the ridiculously attractive involuntary responses, she couldn't guess.

He inhaled deeply through his nose, causing his nostrils to flare, and, God help her, the sight sent billions of tiny bolts of lightning zinging straight to her erogenous zones. She was pathetically hard up when a simple thing like flaring nostrils dissolved her into a puddle of need, but the realization didn't stop her from wondering if he inhaled with the same disciplined power when he fucked.

You have absolutely no chance of finding out.

But then he pulled his gaze from the wall and pierced her with it.

Holy shit. You have a 50 percent chance of finding out, and a zero percent chance of living through it.

That hot, moody stare dropped away, raked her ass, then

ricocheted to the mirror, bounced off her tits, and finally landed back on her face. She mustered up a self-defensive smirk even though it amounted to playing with fire, because in those volatile depths she saw a testosterone-charged version of the same raw lust tormenting her, shot through with a truly impressive amount of steel-eyed resolve.

Could she tip the balance between lust and resolve? Yeah, if she pushed the right button, right now, he'd throw her over the nearest surface and hate-fuck the smirk right off her face.

But then where will you be?

In the unacceptable position of knowing she'd lived up to his insultingly low expectations. Worse, she'd have to withstand a boatload of self-recriminations, and she had plenty of those to deal with already. That realization took care of the smirk. She drew herself up to her full height, which still only put her at his collarbone, and returned his stare. The light gray T-shirt he wore turned his eyes all the more stormy.

He took another deep breath, and finally answered. "You don't pay men to sleep with you. Good. We're on the same page." Then, to her surprise, he added, "In case your ego needs to hear this, Trouble, I know damn well guys fall all over themselves just to get a chance to jack off to the memory of you shooting them down. I watched them do it last night at the bar. What I'm establishing here is that I'm not going to be one of them."

This was her moment to gather up her pride, and she took it. Lifting her chin, plastering a cool smile on her lips, she replied, "No. You're not. Feel free to jack off to the memory of me telling you that."

Her firm rejection earned her a fleeting smile—a silent touché—that managed to make her feel better.

"See? We're on the same page again." He pulled his phone from the pocket of his dark-blue training shorts. "Step over there and stand straight, facing me."

Awareness skittered along her nerve endings as he framed her up on his screen and snapped off shots before she could even adopt a proper pose.

"Okay. Turn to the right."

All of a sudden, the idea of standing in her underwear while he took shot after dispassionate shot made her feel oddly vulnerable. She put a hand on her hip. "You know, it would take less than five minutes for me to run back to the villa and change into something that conforms to your idea of workout attire."

"That would be *my* five minutes, and I'm not willing to forfeit them. When you earn a break, if you want to take five minutes of *your* time to change clothes, that's up to you. Face right."

She turned and rolled her eyes at the far wall. "Okaaaay. When do I get a break?"

"You don't 'get' a break. You 'earn' one. When, depends on you."

Jesus, he was a hard-ass. "So this is some kind of…what? Punishment?"

"It's a consequence. Face the wall."

A consequence that left her stripped down and standing with her nose in the corner like a recalcitrant schoolgirl? Behind her, he clicked away, and she'd never felt more aware of how much skin she had exposed. Her face burned. "Semantics."

"Face left." After she followed his instruction, he continued, "No. A punishment is a penalty inflicted for an offense. A consequence is an outcome resulting from an action. The outcome can be negative, positive, or neutral." He lowered the phone and scrolled through the shots, making selections. "I'm a big believer in consequences."

"People actually pay you for this?"

He didn't look up from the screen, but she saw his lips

twitch. "Yep. In six weeks we'll take 'After' photos and you'll understand why, but for now, let's go over your 'Before' photos."

She'd seen a zillion pictures of herself, in everything from a three-piece tuxedo to a light dusting of bronzer and strategically crossed limbs. Nothing about her own image would surprise her at this point. Confident in that, she stepped over until she stood beside him, looked down at the screen, and—"Oh my God."

"Problem?"

Hell to the yes, there was a problem. Was the woman in the picture really her? Too shocked to ask for permission, she simply took the phone from his hand and scrolled through the shots. All the shots. From every unforgiving angle. Yes, logically, she'd known she'd rounded out a little, but she hadn't really *seen* the difference in the mirror. Aside from enhanced cleavage, her eyes—very unobjective eyes, as it turned out—had seen her old, lean figure staring back at her, and assumed the change was pretty much invisible except to someone like Eddie.

It was not. Not to Eddie, and not to the empirical glare of the camera.

"I look so…soft."

He took his phone back and tapped the screen. "I'm texting these to you. Save them. Put them somewhere handy. I want you to see them every morning."

She never wanted to see those pictures again. "*That's* punishment, making me look at my fat ass every day."

"It's motivation. And to be clear, you're not fat. Your weight and BMI fall within the normal range for your height and age."

"No." She pointed to the picture of her from behind. "That is not normal. This is not how I normally look."

"I'm only going to say this once, Trouble. Here's the

truth—you're at a healthy weight. We can cancel this right now if that's your goal."

"I can't show up on the set looking like this." She gestured down her body. "I signed a contract."

"Yes, you did. And you might want to rethink participating in a business where you can get fired for something as stupid and inconsequential as a change in appearance—"

"I love what I do." She did. He made it sound superficial, summed up in a single contract clause. And some aspects of it were, but crazy demands and relentless scrutiny aside, she loved immersing herself in a role and living in someone else's world for a little while. She loved the intellectual, emotional, and yes, even the physical challenges of embodying a character. Doing it well exercised both logic and creativity. She knew exactly how lucky she was to get paid for following her passion. She didn't take it for granted, and she wasn't going to miss out on the best project to come her way since landing the lead in *Pep Rally* because she couldn't get into shape for the role.

"What you're hoping to do here—get seriously cut in a short amount of time—is one of the least healthy things you can do. It's also hard on you. Over the next weeks, we're going to shock your body into burning fat while simultaneously toning muscles. During that process you'll cycle through fatigue, mood swings, food cravings, headaches, sleeplessness, and a host of other possible side effects, all in the name of bringing your body back to a state I don't understand why you slipped out of in the first place. The results of your medical screenings say there's nothing amiss physically, which means there's something else going on."

"There's nothing going on." Jesus. Why did every conversation have to turn into a psychological evaluation?

"I don't buy that. According to Eddie, you're disciplined and focused when it comes to your career, and yet, on the brink of a major opportunity, you slack off. Maybe you're sabotaging yourself out of a fear of success? Maybe you're rebelling against someone's expectations? I really don't know, and six weeks isn't enough time to figure it out. If anyone except Eddie had asked me to take you on, I would have said no, because I don't believe in this. Enabling a binge and purge mentality is not what I do."

Every word that came out of his mouth offended her. She hadn't binged. Not really. She hadn't slacked. Not willfully. Her current situation wasn't the result of some subconscious self-sabotage, or passive-aggressive rebellion. She'd been forced to park her ass on a couch for the better part of eight weeks, doing only the approved physical therapy while her knee healed. But mentioning the knee injury pried the top off a can of worms she didn't want to open in front of anyone—particularly not a man who already considered her trouble. Confiding painful details of her family life to Luke McLean wasn't part of the deal. She *wanted* to tell him that if he was so damn conflicted about taking her on, he could just leave her a few workout routines, a manageable diet, and go back to California. But she didn't dare, now that she'd gotten a true gander at herself. Attaining the physique to play Lena Xavier was going to take more than thirty minutes on the elliptical machine every morning. She needed his help.

"You know what? Let's leave my head out of this. I get that you have better things to do and more worthy people to do them with, but you signed a contract, too. A generous one, I think you'd agree, since you dictated the terms. You committed to help me get back in shape, quickly and safely. That's all we need to concentrate on. I need you and your expertise to be ready for this role."

He regarded her for a long moment, brows knitted in the default scowl he always seemed to wear when he looked at her, but defining the cause of this particular scowl presented a challenge. Was he pissed at her for telling him she expected him to do what he'd signed on to do? The silence stretched so long, she heard the trilling call of some tropical bird outside, and the answering call from its buddy, or possibly its mate. At least some creatures were communicating well.

Finally, he cupped his hand behind his ear. "Say the last bit again, Trouble, a little louder."

What the…? She reran her words in her mind. "I…uh…I need you and your expertise—"

"There." He pointed at her. "That first part. Louder, please."

Now she saw it. The trace of a self-satisfied smile on his lips. Dammit, he'd manipulated her again. While she thought she'd been putting him in his place, he'd been leading her exactly to this admission, and it was too late to take it back. She rolled her eyes, but gave him his due. "I need you."

"*Louder.*" He raised his voice to demonstrate. The birds outside abandoned the courtyard in a frenzy of squawks and the flap of wings.

God save her, she had to do it. And he knew it. She closed her eyes to block out his smug, unfairly handsome face, drew in a deep breath to fill her lungs, and let it rip like a cadet at boot camp. "I. Need. You."

The words echoed off the walls and reverberated in her head for several heartbeats. Silence eventually washed in, uncomfortably loud in the wake of her outburst, and made her aware of other details. She was breathing fast, panting as if she'd sprinted up a flight of stairs instead of just yelled three little words. Sweat coated her upper lip. Her knuckles ached from clenching her fists so tightly.

The silence drew out, forcing her to acknowledge more of her body's reactions. Her breasts felt heavy, swollen, and unbearably constrained by her workout bra. Her nipples stung from standing at attention, and muscles deep inside her contracted so hard, her thighs trembled.

Her forehead and cheeks burned.

If he was still wearing the shit-eating grin when she opened her eyes, she was going to have to sucker punch him, even though he was twice her size and she'd probably break her hand if she landed the shot. But when she opened her eyes there was no hint of the smile. Or the scowl. His expression was neutral, and yet…there was a trace of something in his eyes. Some mesmerizing intensity that told her he knew exactly what effect submitting to his demands and admitting her need had on her, and warned her he wasn't unscathed, either.

His lips parted.

She held her breath.

"Okay, Trouble. Let's get started."

• • •

He might have told Quinn working out in her underwear was a consequence rather than a punishment, but it qualified as pure punishment for him. Watching her breasts bounce and her ass jiggle as she pounded out a three mile warm-up on the treadmill tortured his cock as effectively as if she'd been trying to make him hurt.

God help him if she ever actually tried. He'd have her over the console of that treadmill so fast, she'd never even manage a cry of surprise. He'd leave her clinging there, legs dangling, feet scrambling for toeholds along the motor cover while he dragged the panties aside and sank into her heat. Then she'd cry out—another wall-rattling *I need you,* as long as he was fantasizing—and take him in deeper as her grip on the console wavered and her body slid down onto his. He'd fold his hands over hers and fuck her back up to her original position, let her slide down, and repeat the whole thing until her arms shook from the strain. Until her spine arched, her glutes tightened, and she screamed *I need you* at the top of her lungs, squeezing his soul out of him through his cock while she bucked and trembled her way through yet another consequence.

Client. Actress. Smart-ass. Three strikes, McLean. You're out. He turned away and adjusted himself as discretely as a guy could in a room where mirrors dominated the walls. A small, glass-fronted refrigerator tucked under a counter at the other end of the room caught his eye. He headed over and took out a bottle of water. She'd be desperate for hydration by the end of the warm-up. As he made his way back to her, however, he had to give credit where credit was due. She'd ranked running as one of her least favorite activities in the preferences questionnaire she'd completed prior to arrival. On top of that, champagne produced a gnarly hangover, and the energy from the refined sugars she'd consumed last night was long gone by now. But she hadn't uttered a word of complaint. She gutted it out.

She also favored her left leg. Just a little, but she'd been doing it from the start. It was no better, or worse, now that she was—he drew up alongside the machine and checked the readout—2.87 miles into the warm-up. Still, the detail merited some follow-up, because she hadn't divulged any injuries in her health questionnaires. He twisted the cap on the water bottle and placed it in the holder built into the treadmill's console. She cast the water a longing look, but didn't reach for the bottle.

Okay. They'd talk first. "Last night you mentioned you'd gotten derailed a couple months ago and had to take a break from your normal workouts." He raised his voice to be heard over the hum of the machine. "Tell me about that."

"Nothing to tell. I was just making conversation."

He found her eyes in the mirror and stared her down.

"Last night I mentioned a very important requirement of our deal. Do you remember?"

"Did you?" She frowned, but he thought she might be feigning the confusion.

"It had to do with honesty."

She reached for the water now, and took a long swallow. Buying time. She'd rather show that little weakness of accepting something from him than reveal whatever had derailed her. The treadmill wasn't cooperating, though. It beeped, signaling the end of the warm-up he'd programmed. Her eyes darted to the readout panel, and then up to him—face-to-face this time rather than via the mirror. "You told me not to lie to you again or..." She paused for breath. "... no deal."

The pace of the running belt slowed to the point she could walk. The beauty of the treadmill was no matter how fast or slow she moved, she couldn't outrun this conversation. He had her hemmed in. "Good to know it's not all a blur. Here's the thing, Trouble. When I ask you a question, I need an honest answer because it all factors into how I'm going to accomplish your goals, safely. If I can't rely on you to be straight with me, then I can't be certain what we're doing here is safe for you. And I won't work under those conditions. So, let's try this again." The treadmill stopped. He unclipped the shutoff key from the waist of her underwear and ordered his fingers not to linger on her smooth, damp skin. "Something derailed you a couple months ago?"

She held his gaze for another second, then sighed and slumped against the rail on the other side of the machine—as far from him as she could get without doing something drastic—and rubbed the back of her neck. "I hurt my knee. It's not a big deal, but I had to take it easy for awhile."

"Elaborate on 'hurt.'"

Her eyes narrowed a little at his tone, but he didn't really care. He asked clients to complete the health questionnaires for a reason.

"I sprained it, but it's completely—"

"ACL?"

She shook her head. "MCL."

"Grade?"

"Grade 3, but it's completely healed. I swear." She leaned forward now, hands wrapped around the rail between them, talking fast. "I got the MRI. I wore the brace. I kept it elevated, and completed weeks of PT. I have no pain, and full range of motion. My orthopedist cleared me to return to my regular routine. I didn't lie on your precious questionnaire. I have no medical conditions that would prevent me from doing any type of physical exercise."

Unfortunately, by her own account, that *wasn't* what her orthopedist said. "According to your doc, you have no medical condition that would prevent you from returning to your regular routine. Did your regular routine include running between six and ten miles a day, kickboxing, power yoga, and weight training?"

"Six to ten miles of running a *day*? Are you serious?"

Not surprisingly, the mention of the non-preferred activity got a reaction out of her, but he was serious about all of it. "Few things melt fat faster. Your role requires you be lean *and* muscular. When it comes right down to it, you need your dancer's body back, but fast. You don't have months to spend regaining the strength and flexibility, so along with the cardio, I'll layer in weight training to add definition and some fight training to get you moving like an ass kicker, which will make your director happy. Basically, Quinn, I designed these next six weeks as a high-intensity, keep-your-body guessing, tour-de-force, and now I'm concerned you can't handle it."

"I can handle anything. Dancing is like all that stuff rolled into one, and my knee is fine." She wrapped one hand high around the vertical support bar of the functional trainer, balanced on her left foot, and wrapped the other hand around her right ankle. Then she proceeded to lift her right leg up. Sweet Jesus, all the way up…into a standing split. Graceful as a ballerina, she pointed her toes to the ceiling. With one brow cocked, she looked at him. "See?"

All he could see was her assuming the same pose, naked, while clinging to his bedpost.

"Impressive," he managed to say, and kicked the wandering part of his brain back into line. Yes, he could take some comfort from the fact that her "regular routine" was pretty physical, but still. This added uncertainty, and he hated uncertainty. "But forgive me if I don't rely on the Quinn Sheridan School of Health Management. Come here." He walked to the weight bench she'd almost tripped over earlier. "Take a seat." Once she settled herself on the padded bench, he knelt in front of her and gently palpated around her kneecap with this thumbs, using his fingers to feel along the back of her joint where the medial collateral ligament attached. "Any pain?" He watched her face as he asked.

"None. I told you, I'm fine."

Her expression backed up her words. He saw no twinges of discomfort. He straightened her leg, then took hold of her shin just above her ankle and spanned his other hand across her thigh. The muscles there jumped at his touch. He froze. "Does that hurt?"

"No." The word came out softly, a little breathlessly, and made him instantly aware of the warm, smooth skin beneath his palm. His hand looked huge, tan and rugged against the pale silk of her thigh. His fingers had only a short journey to reach softer, warmer flesh protected by a flimsy layer of Lycra. She released a shuddery breath and relaxed her body. Her legs splayed open slightly in what his dick wanted to read as an invitation.

One you can't accept.

He cleared his throat and yanked his mind out of her panties. "Resist me." He applied careful pressure, slowly pushing her leg down against the opposition of her quads. The joint held. Encouraged, he slid his hand a few inches higher on her shin and loosened his arm a degree. "Extend." This time he provided the resistance while she flexed her knee until her leg was once again parallel to the floor. "No pain?"

"No pain."

"Okay." He guided her leg back to its natural position. "Your quads aren't protesting. That's a good sign."

"It's the sign of a perfectly healthy knee." She crossed her arms as she spoke, unintentionally—or hell, maybe intentionally—taunting him with the sight of her breasts all but spilling out of her top.

He swallowed the urge to sink his teeth into the opulent flesh. Bite her like a ripe peach, and then smooth the mark away with his tongue. She could have a real problem here, for Christ's sake. "If your knee is perfectly healthy, why are you babying it?"

Her eyebrows shot up. The question clearly caught her by surprise. "I'm not."

"You favor your other leg when you run. It could be psychological or physiological. You had an injury, and your body learned to compensate by taking more weight on the left leg. But at this point, I don't know if it's a habit, or a sign that your knee isn't one hundred percent. Flip over and lie flat on the bench. I want to test your range of motion."

And stop staring at your tits like a sweaty-palmed pervert.

"My range of motion is normal."

"Prove it."

She shot him an indignant look. He returned it unflinchingly. Over the next six weeks, he was going to push her right to her breaking point mentally and physically, but he didn't want to *hurt* her. He needed to be sure nothing he had in store for her would come close.

Apparently he convinced her he wasn't going to back down on this, because she swiveled and brought her legs up onto the bench. Then, agile as a cat, she flipped onto her stomach, and stretched, wiggling her hips a little as if to find a comfortable position. Finally, she stilled. With her arms folded and supporting her chin, she managed to come across like a spa patron about to be serviced.

He leaned over her, wrapped one hand around her ankle, and prepared to brace the other at the base of her spine. And that's when he realized facing down her cleavage was the lesser of two evils. Her ass embodied everything about her that worked his shit in two proud, irresistible handfuls—a seductive, defiant challenge just begging for some proper attention.

If he had the right to touch her intimately for pleasure, this is where he'd leave his mark. Each time she allowed him the privilege, in some new way, until she presented to him eagerly just to see what he did next. She shifted on the bench, inching her body up in a move that lifted her hips invitingly, and saliva filled the back of his mouth. He swallowed, and brought his molars together with an audible click.

"I'm ready." Her husky voice feathered along his nerve endings.

Still gritting his teeth, he placed his hand along the top of her panties and bent her leg to a ninety-degree angle. "Tell me immediately if this starts to hurt."

"You're not hurting me."

"And I don't want to"—he inched her leg to a deeper angle—"so speak up if I reach your limit."

"Keep going. I think you'll find my limits are very flexible."

The inflection in her voice told him she knew exactly

where his mind was going with that response. So be it. The rest of him couldn't tag along. He folded her leg back…and back…and back until he pressed her heel against the bottom half of one smooth, pale cheek. At that point hormones gave over to awe. "Jesus, you're limber."

"I've danced since I was a kid."

It was not the response of someone in agony. Still, he asked, "Any discomfort?"

"Not in my knee."

When he glanced up, she had her head resting on her shoulder, so her sardonic smile greeted him.

How the fuck was he going to survive her? Desperate to focus on something besides the air crackling like static between them, he eased her leg back.

She winced. A fleeting sign of discomfort, but he saw it.

"That does it." He pretty much lifted her off the bench and set her on her feet. "Get dressed."

"What? Why?"

"I want a second opinion."

Chapter Five

When Quinn returned to the patient lounge to find Luke sitting in the midst of the calming blue and white room, it occurred to her that nobody had accompanied her to a medical appointment in a very long time. She'd dealt with the sprained knee quietly, on her own, not wanting the press, or worse, the *Dirty Games* producers, to find out about the injury.

Hollywood was a cutthroat place. Most everyone worked an angle, but Quinn found an almost refreshing honesty to the naked ambition. She'd played the game long enough to know the score. Confidences had an uncanny tendency to find their way into the spotlight. She couldn't afford for her dirtiest laundry—the ugly facts surrounding her knee injury, or her current situation—to be hung out for public view. Those details would hamper Callum's attempts to get clean and get his career back on track, and could send hers off the rails as well, if the producers panicked about her fitness for the role. Eddie, she trusted, but even then, not with everything. The need for extreme discretion had narrowed her support network considerably. Like, to herself. She wasn't used to having someone in her corner at times like this.

Luke wasn't there out of friendship, or to offer support, but still, seeing his imposing frame parked in a chair waiting for her was strangely reassuring. Watching his miss-no-detail eyes scan her face for any sign of distress left an unaccountably warm feeling in her chest. She crossed the room and lowered herself into the seat beside him.

"How'd it go?" He looked completely relaxed with his arm slung across the back of the blue, upholstered chairs, and his right ankle propped on his left knee. He held out the cell phone she'd given him to hold while she'd spent thirty minutes in an MRI suite being crammed into a magnetic tube where metallic items were prohibited.

She took the phone and shrugged, trying to muster up a breezy response when, in truth, thirty minutes of lying there while the machine did its thing had sucked away her energy. A mellow fog she associated with lack of sleep blanketed her. "Fine. The technician said the results would be ready in about twenty minutes."

His eyes narrowed. "Did they give you a Xanax or something?"

"Oh for God's sake. *No.* I don't suffer from anxiety. I'm not a basket case, despite what you think."

"Hey, a lot of people get claustrophobic in the tube, or they don't like the noise. That hardly makes you a basket case."

"Well, I was only waist deep in the machine, and I wore headphones to block out the banging. I'm not drugged. Just tired." And hungry. And grumpy.

To cover the yawn trying to slip out, she craned her neck and looked around the otherwise empty room. Comfortable and upscale, just like the resort this cutting edge wellness center served. A guest could come to Paradise Bay for anything from an extreme makeover to a stem cell treatment, and recover in the comfort of the adjacent resort.

A flat screen along one wall was tuned to a daytime talk show. The magazines scattered on the dark wood tables between the chair groupings focused on fashion, celebrity gossip, or parenting. Not a *Men's Health* in the bunch. She couldn't imagine him finding any of it remotely interesting. "You must have been bored out of your mind."

He tapped the screen of his own phone and slid it into his pocket. "I managed." When he withdrew his hand his fist was closed, and she realized he'd retrieved the earrings she'd also given him to look after. She held out her hand for them, but he ignored it, and pulled the back off one of the diamond forget-me-not studs Callum had given her when she'd won the lead role on *Pep Rally*. Back then, he'd still had money to spend on a sweet, brotherly gesture of support. Those days were long gone. Now he needed her support, and she needed this role in order to continue to provide it.

But then all thoughts of Callum or anything else fled, because Luke leaned close. The sunburst of amber around his pupils captured her attention. Faceted, like a tiger's eye, and every bit as mesmerizing. Tiny rivers of gold streamed through the winter lake pools of his irises, presenting a contradiction of hot and cold, wild and contained, just like the man himself. She held her breath while he eased the post through her earlobe, and then locked the back into place. While he inserted and secured the other earring, she had a sudden, unaccountably vivid image of him biting the earrings out. Using his teeth to divest her of all adornments. Tear away every trapping of civility. Every tiny defense. She shuddered, and imagined him using the same attentive, oh-so-meticulous care to find and exploit her most repressed needs.

All the tightly strung warning systems inside her went lax. She swallowed, ordered herself to stop staring at him, and managed to drag her gaze away from his fascinating eyes. Instead, it dropped to his mouth. Not necessarily a better choice. His lips looked firm and capable. Enticingly mobile, especially as they formed a word.

They paused, expectantly, and she realized he'd asked her a question.

"Huh?"

She could almost imagine the taste of his lips. There wasn't an ounce of softness to him, but if she crashed her mouth against his, those lips would give. And then they'd take. They'd part, and the very act would force hers open, too. Open and vulnerable, and…

"Hungry?" As he repeated the question, he reached into a bag at his feet and pulled out a square box. "I ordered lunch while you were gone."

She had to pull her slack mouth closed to respond. "Thanks." Mentally shaking herself, she accepted the beige box. Just holding it reminded her she was hungry. Starving, actually. Her hands shook a little as she popped the top of the cardboard clamshell to reveal… *Oh nooooo.* "What is this?"

"Grilled chicken and kale salad." He handed her napkin-wrapped plastic utensils and a bottle of water before adding, "Bon appetite." Then he popped the lid on his container.

The spicy aroma of something mouthwatering surrounded her. He dug in and lifted a forkful of rice drowned in a sauce chocked full of peppers, onions, and God only knew what other goodness. Her stomach growled.

"I want what you're having."

He took an unrepentant bite, and closed his eyes to savor the flavor. Finally, he swallowed and shook his head. "Nope. Sofrito is not on your approved diet for the next six weeks. Neither is rice, for that matter." So saying, he enjoyed another bite.

"Why not? I see peppers in there, and onion—"

"And carbs. Carbs my body needs for energy. You need to burn through your body's stored energy reserves, which means we restrict calories and make every single one of them meaningful. Lean protein will account for most of yours. Fiber from green vegetables like spinach, kale, and broccoli will help you feel full. No processed food. No added sugars." His gaze turned pointed. "No alcohol for the duration. I trust *that's* not going to be a problem."

None whatsoever. After this morning, she didn't care if she never drank again. She gave his sofrito one last look, and then stared at her joyless chicken on its bed of roughage. "When I filled out the meal questionnaire, I indicated there were three things I couldn't live without. Starbucks, chocolate, and ice cre—"

"No, no, and no."

"None of it for six weeks?" Even she heard the whine in her voice.

"I penciled in two treats. One when you hit the halfway point—if you make it that long—and one when we're done. Again, if—"

"Yeah, yeah, yeah." She batted the disclaimer away with a wave of her hand. "Thank you for your vote of confidence."

He ignored her interruption. "Otherwise, you eat what I say, when I say. And it's going to look a lot like this." He pointed to her lunch. "Understood?"

Fuuuuck. For an answer she sawed off a chunk of chicken, stabbed it onto her fork along with a leaf of kale, and shoved it in her mouth. Forcing herself to chew took more effort, but somehow she managed.

"Good." His lips lifted in a grin, and he helped himself to more of his lunch.

Don't complain. She took another bite of her chicken and chewed. He expected her to complain, and she wouldn't give him the satisfaction of…"God, does it have to be so…

boring?"

"The purpose of this food is to nourish your body, not entertain you. Entertain yourself with books, activities, conversations—"

"Okay, then. Let's talk." Figuring she might as well know the extent of her losses for the next six weeks, she went with, "What other basic human rights have I surrendered to you, besides the ability to choose what I eat, and what I wear? Oh, and when I wake up."

His lips quirked. "You can wake up any time you like, as long as it gets you to the gym at nine a.m. I own you from then until we're done for the day, with the exception of two fifteen minute breaks—provided you earn them—and lunch."

Days on the set started earlier, and frequently ran very late. She knew how to put in long hours, but spending so much time, one-on-one, with him gave her a slight rush of panic. "I need a definite end time. I didn't put my entire life on hold when I boarded a plane for Paradise Bay."

"Me, either. I still have a business to oversee, and I'll be doing it long distance for six weeks. We'll knock off each day around three p.m.—give or take—and you can run back to your villa and call your boyfriend, or—"

"I'm not involved with anyone," she said through gritted teeth, just managing to hold back the *you big jerk* dancing on the tip of her tongue. "But I have lines to learn, scripts to read, calls to return. I realize you don't find my job terribly worthwhile, but you're not the only one with other obligations."

Obligations, and a vacation he'd shuffled as a favor to his friend, which must have been painfully inconvenient. The question she'd been dying to ask since the day he'd agreed to train her resurfaced. "What massive debt do you owe Eddie, that he could guilt you into this?"

Luke nodded to indicate he'd heard her, then swallowed

and took a drink of water. Then he said the name of an A-list actress.

"I don't understand. What's she got to do with anything?"

"When I first started out as a personal trainer, I worked for a very well-established guy who had a lot of industry clients. More than he could handle, actually, because they're all insanely demanding. Anyway," he continued when she would have interrupted to stick up for the fellow members of her craft, "I met Eddie through him, and ended up becoming his trainer. We got along. This was a decade ago, and we were both at similar stages in our respective careers. He brought her to one of our sessions. She was his boss's client at the time, and up for a big role. He thought she might benefit from working out regularly, but she was resistant so he used me as bait."

She nearly choked on a mouthful of water. "Bait? She's a human being, not a mantle fish."

He shook his head. "It says more about me than it does her. I was young, eager to make a name for myself in a competitive field, and easily caught up in what seemed, at the time, like a very accomplished person's life. There I was, a redneck kid from Crooked Creek, Texas, who'd ridden a football scholarship to Southern California, and then transitioned that into an exercise science degree when I blew out my ankle halfway through my second year. She was beautiful, successful, and sexy as hell, and suddenly I was moving in her sphere. After a few one-on-one sessions, I was in her bed. Six months later, she asked me to take her on full-time—drop my other clients so I could travel with her, accompany her on set, and focus exclusively on her. She needed me."

A hot emotion she didn't care to identify burned through her blood. He'd taken pains to tell *her* they weren't going to mix business with pleasure, but he obviously did it sometimes.

For the right woman. "Did you?"

"Rookie move." His quick laugh held very little amusement. "I was such a fucking amateur. She'd never looked better, and was a walking advertisement for my services, so my client list was growing by leaps and bounds. But yes, like the dumb-ass twenty-two-year-old I was, I agreed to her request. Eddie warned me not to, but I didn't listen."

The quick storm of heat subsided a little. "What happened?"

"Predictable story. I made her my priority, but she didn't do the same. Any plans I attempted always took a backseat to her career. I ranked behind her agent, her manager, and her publicist, and every one of us knew it. She had a lot of demands on her, but God forbid I suggest I needed more to be happy than to simply hang out in her life. Saying that amounted to a betrayal in her eyes."

"Wow. Basically, 'Be here for me, on my terms, or you're a bad person'? You must have been incredibly hurt."

"I was fucking miserable," he said with such blunt honesty, her heart actually twisted for him. "I couldn't give her what she wanted and still respect myself. It took a few cycles of teary arguments and hurled accusations, but eventually I thought we reached a mutual decision to call it quits. I walked away feeling like we'd treated each other decently, other than the fact that she hadn't actually paid me in months, but whatever. I could get work. Except I couldn't. I contacted all those people who'd begged me to take them on and got nothing but silence."

Okay, yes, he'd been naive, but still, fury rose on his behalf. "She blackballed you?"

He nodded. "I finally called Eddie. He asked around and found out she'd badmouthed me to everyone short of the press. None of those contacts I'd made would touch me with a ten-foot pole. I was facing the possibility of having to pull up stakes, and head home to disappointed looks from my parents, friends…an entire town that thought I was living a fast, glamorous life out in Cali, full of people they only saw on TV or in the pages of magazines. Instead, they'd know I'd been chewed up and spit out, in large part because of my own ego and stupidity. Thankfully, Eddie didn't let that happen. He quietly referred a few up-and-coming clients my way, mostly on the sports side of his business. I got results, earned favorable word-of-mouth, and rebuilt my career. If it weren't for him risking backlash from one of his firm's biggest clients, I'd have been back to square one. He went out on a limb for me after I did something boneheaded, and I owed him."

She swallowed that information, along with the final bite of chicken. "Is she the reason you don't like working with actors?"

He laughed and put his lunch aside. "She didn't have quite that much sway over me. I've worked with scores of actors over the years. Sports and entertainment clients made up most of my business for a long time. Some have been amazing, others frustrating. I *do* credit her with teaching me a valuable lesson about mixing my professional life with my personal life."

An impulse to argue his conclusion gripped her. *Not your business.* "So, if your experience with her didn't put you off this industry, what did?"

"Don't take it personally."

Now she laughed. "Pfft. Of course not. Why would I take your utter lack of esteem for my chosen profession personally?"

"Because it's not directed at you, but it's personal to me. About five years ago, at the request of a client who was involved with a charity for injured armed forces personnel, I took on a vet who had lost a leg in the line of duty. He'd struggled with weight since the injury, and had just been diagnosed with type-two diabetes. This guy wasn't after washboard abs or a V-cut. He didn't give a shit about looking good for the camera. He needed to get control of his blood sugar, and reclaim his health.

"It wasn't easy, but we did it, and working with him changed me as fundamentally as it changed him. His determination energized me, and reminded me I had the skills to help people make life-altering improvements. I could continue to use those skills to line my pockets even though I'd started to question the value of my work, or I could get a new goal in place and set about making changes of my own. Over the following years, I took on more clients with substantial health challenges. Training athletes and celebrities pays well—"

"No kidding." She still got a serious cramp in the vicinity of her wallet when she thought about the cost of this six-week boot camp.

"The money allowed me to buy a facility, add staff, and concentrate on clients with serious weight management issues and all the accompanying complications. We don't merely offer physical training. It's everything—diet, habits, mindset—we help identify and tackle all the obstacles between the individual and their optimal health. We're small, but we're good, and we get results. Even so, it's taken a lot of energy and focus to evolve the business to where it is today. I have a great team in place, and a comfortably full roster of clients. I'm finally at the point where I could consider stepping back for some personal time."

Well, damn. Now that she knew his situation, his arrogance started to seem more like the genuine frustration of a man caught between a need to recharge, and his vow to a friend. She didn't really know what to say. "Just so you know, I didn't ask Eddie to—"

The waiting room door swung upon with a squeak, and then someone drew in an audible breath.

"Holyyy Shiiittt. You're Quinn Sheridan!"

Chapter Six

The outburst came from a guy, sixteen or seventeen if Luke had to guess, who stood in the doorway next to a woman who wore a facility ID around her neck.

"Joshua, wait," the woman admonished as the kid made a beeline for Quinn.

Luke leaned forward in his chair and prepared to stand. Occasional bodyguard duty came with the territory, and currently, he was the only thing protecting Quinn from unwanted attention. But her hand landed on his forearm, signaling him back. She sent him a restraining look before turning a full-wattage smile on the kid. "Hi. Something tells me you're a *Pep Rally* fan."

"Massive fan." He nudged the nurse now standing beside him. "Camilla here can tell you. Me, and most of the other kids in my program, watch the show every week. We're bummed this is the final season."

"Becky was a lot of fun to play. I'm glad you enjoyed the show." She held out her hand to Camilla. "I'm Quinn."

The woman took her hand. "Nice to meet you. I'm a

patient escort for the wellness center. And this is Josh. I'm supposed to be keeping him in check..."

Josh rolled his eyes at that, but Camilla sent him a grin before adding, "I hope we're not disturbing you."

"Not at all." Quinn patted the seat next to her. "Please, sit. This is my...friend, Luke."

He greeted them, and then sat back and listened as Josh told her how "righteously hot" she was, and how his friends were never going to believe he'd met her. She offered to take a picture with him, but he explained he'd had to surrender his electronics as part of his intake process—he was on Paradise Bay to complete a ninety-day rehab program. Quinn digested that without blinking, and told him she was there preparing for a role.

"I know. You're going to be Lena fucking Xavier! Me and my friends at home play *Dirty Games* all the time. We've like, hit the level cap. It's our favorite."

"I hope we can do it justice on the big screen."

"You're going to kick ass." In the way of excited, hormonal teens everywhere, he peppered Quinn with questions. What was going to happen on the final season of *Pep Rally?* Was so-and-so going to end up with so-and-so? Did she ever date fans?

She answered with easy humor, insisting she couldn't tell him any *Pep Rally* spoilers or she'd have to kill him, and she hadn't had time to date anyone lately.

Luke silently reminded himself that last piece of information was none of his concern.

Quinn also delicately asked a few questions of her own, and discovered Josh lived in Southern California, but had come to Paradise Bay for rehab. Second attempt. The first effort, back home, hadn't stuck. She didn't follow him too far down that hole. Instead, she simply asked him how he was feeling, and offered congratulations when he proudly announced he'd earned his sixty-day chip.

Most people encountering a kid Josh's age asked about future plans—college, career—stuff like that, but Quinn didn't. Instincts, or maybe some personal experience, told her he had enough on his plate just getting through the next month. She kept things in the moment, focusing on the island. Had he been to the beach? Snorkeled?

The sensitivity with which she handled Josh's situation, his adulation—all of it—wasn't cautious or awkward, and Luke couldn't help but admire the seemingly genuine, and relentlessly positive way she interacted with a young fan at such a complicated place in his life. Respect did have to be earned, but she was earning some of his with this encounter. When a nurse appeared at the door and announced the doctor was ready to review her MRI results, Quinn handed Josh a card she slipped out of a pocket on her phone sleeve.

"This is my agent's number. When you get back to Cali, call him, and he'll arrange for you to visit the *Dirty Games* set. Bring your ninety-day chip with you, because I want to see it. We'll get pictures then, okay?"

Josh was stoked, to say the least. He took the card, and a hug. As Quinn followed the nurse through the door and down the hall to the doctor's office, Luke whispered, "You just gave that kid the best incentive any therapist could offer to get him to complete his program."

Quinn's answering smile was startlingly bittersweet. "While it would be nice to think I could be so effective with nothing more than my good intentions, I know that's not the case. The biggest key to Josh's recovery is Josh. We'll see." She shrugged, but it fell short of noncommittal. "I am rooting for him."

Yeah, there was definitely more to dig into here. She'd been touched by addiction. Maybe a friend, or a family member, or…maybe her? His gut tightened at the thought.

They'd delve into the topic later, when they had privacy. For now, he followed her into the orthopedist's office and leaned against the windowsill while the congenial, middle-aged man confirmed her MCL, and knee as a whole, looked good. He recommended using a brace if she felt like she needed lateral support, and mentioned that the pharmacy carried a wide selection if she didn't already have one.

Luke aimed a questioning look at her. She frowned and shook her head. "I used one during the initial phase of PT, but I didn't bring it with me. I haven't needed it in weeks."

"Looks like we'll be stopping at the pharmacy."

"I don't need a brace," she said under her breath as they left the medical office.

"You don't need to reinjure your knee." He held the door to the pharmacy and ushered her inside.

After explaining to the clerk what they were looking for, she showed them to the sports brace section, and invited Quinn to try on any that interested her. Then she retreated to assist another customer. Luke pointed to one of the two chairs the shop had placed in the section. "Sit."

"I'm not a German shepherd," she huffed, but sat anyway. He scanned the options, looking for something simple and streamlined, and selected three possibilities.

"I like that one," she said as he knelt in front of her and placed the choices on the chair beside her. Picking it up, she inspected it more closely. "It's much smaller than the one I had."

He took it out of her hands and unfastened the straps. "We're going down a level from what you probably used. You don't need the same degree of support anymore."

"I don't need any support. Hey—" She stiffened as he pushed the leg of her sweatpants up to midthigh. "What are you doing?"

"Putting it on. I want to see how it fits, and I want you

to move and tell me how it feels." As he spoke, he slipped the brace around her knee and secured the lower Velcro strap. Tight. Unwanted images infiltrated his mind. Quinn, sprawled across his bed, with her wrists strapped to his headboard, and her ankles tethered to his bedposts. A quick inhale brought his head up in time to see awareness flicker in her eyes.

He secured the top strap, and tugged the brace a little to test its give. "Are you comfortable?"

She cleared her throat. "Yes. Um. I don't know. Maybe it's a little snug?"

"We're after a secure bind. Secure, but I don't want you to feel overly restrained." He forced himself to blink, break the trance they'd both slipped into. The effort wasn't entirely successful, especially when she replied, "I think I can handle this level of restraint."

He traced the top seam of the brace around to the delicate skin at the inside of her thigh. "I'm going to ask you to stand and do a few exercises in a moment. Concentrate on how it feels here, because this area is vulnerable to chafing."

"Oh." Her breath left her lungs in a little gust that ruffled the hair at his temple, and her back sagged into the chair. "Is it?"

He looked up into slumberous blue eyes. Without really meaning to, he pressed his thumb into the soft flesh. A deep muscle quivered and released. Every part of his body tightened. "It can be. I want to address your specific needs, but not with something too punishing."

Her hand drifted down her thigh, fingertips stopping just short of where his rested. "That's right. You don't believe in punishment."

"I never said that."

Her lashes snapped up, and her eyes locked on his. "You said...consequences."

"I merely drew a distinction between punishment and consequence. If I were to punish you, Trouble, it would be a very deliberate, very unmistakable thing. There would be absolutely no question in your mind about what was happening to you, or why. It would not be a careless act, and while you might experience certain aftereffects"—he rubbed his thumb along her skin, right above the brace—"I guarantee you an abrasion wouldn't be one of them."

She slid forward in the chair, and he lowered his head a notch. Maybe she wouldn't notice he was fantasizing about burying his face between her legs?

It took her two quick inhales to catch her breath. "I'm tougher than I look. Nobody who knows me thinks I'm fragile."

Jesus, he had to get ahold of himself. He shook his head to clear it at as much as to refute her statement. "Parts of you are." He cupped the back of her knee and honed in on the question she'd skirted with him, and the doctor. She'd characterized her injury, been detailed about the type and degree of the sprain, but she hadn't disclosed the cause. His instincts nagged at him to ask. He looked into her beautifully unguarded face. "How'd it happen, Quinn?"

Something shuttered behind her eyes. She looked away. "I fell."

"An MCL sprain is a contact injury. I see it with football players, soccer players. Clients involved in tackle sports." He took her chin and turned her face back to his. "Did somebody take you down?"

She was already shaking her head when she opened her mouth. "I—"

"Remember rule number one," he interjected. "Don't lie to me."

Wrong tactic. Her chin went up, along with all her defenses. "I'm not. Look, Luke, you already know everything you need to know about my knee. You're not my insurance company. I don't owe you an accident report."

So much for instincts. He had to pick his battles with Quinn, and the truth was, he didn't want to draw a line in the sand over this. Not yet, anyway. He got to his feet and walked to the display wall, leaving an open area between them. "Sounds like we're done talking, then. Let's put this brace to the test." He pointed to the space. "Come over here and give me ten four-count burpees."

If looks could kill, he'd be getting sized for a body bag right now. But despite her mutinous expression, she stood, walked to the center of the floor, and prepared to do as he asked.

"Oh, and Quinn?"

She expelled a loud breath and turned to shoot lasers at him with those baby blues. "What?"

"I'm tougher than I look, too."

• • •

"I'm thinking the fact that you answered my call means you're not still mad at me, eh, Quinnie?"

Quinn heard a note of contrition beneath her brother's forcefully upbeat question and warned herself not to drop her guard completely. Drugs or no, Callum was an excellent actor. "I'm not mad at you."

"Even though I trashed your life?"

Although she stood alone in the kitchen of her villa, the instinct to take precautions against anyone overhearing anything about her brother's situation kicked in. Maybe, as twins, they felt extra protective of each other, or maybe watching him grow up in the spotlight had done it, but guarding his privacy came as naturally as guarding her own. She used the towel draped over her shoulder to wipe sweat from a relentless morning of cardio off her face, and then switched the call from speaker and brought her phone to her ear. "You didn't trash my life." Aspects of it were a little worse for wear, but nothing she couldn't repair. Hopefully. "How are you?"

"I'm okay." A self-deprecating laugh flowed over the line. "Rehab sucks, even in this country club you've sprung for, but I'm feeling better. More stable. Much more in control."

"Good to know." She hated the caution in her response, but dealing with Callum the last several months had trained her to be wary. The days when there had been no need for careful words and safe topics seemed like another lifetime. She missed hanging out on set with him when they were little, plotting escapes from stern, old Mrs. Frick, their tutor, in between taping his scenes as the precocious, what-will-pop-out-of-his-mouth-next kid in the family-oriented sitcom that had put him on the map. Hearing old Eminem songs could bring tears to her eyes, remembering how they'd filled downtime making their mom film "videos" of them rapping and dancing to "Slim Shady" or "Lose Yourself." When she'd get depressed about a botched audition or a lost role, he'd talk like Yoda or Forrest Gump just to make her laugh.

"What's wrong? Aren't you happy to talk to me? Shit. You are mad, aren't you?"

"No. I just…I didn't expect to hear from you." She opened the fridge and looked for today's lunch box from the resort. Luke preordered all her meals, snacks, and drinks, so they'd be ready and waiting for her at the proper times. Five days into her training, she already knew a meal break was nothing to squander. Her stomach growled in protest at the empty shelves. Dang. They hadn't delivered her lunch yet. She'd have to call the concierge when she finished talking to her brother. "You were pretty resistant to going to Foundations. I thought *you* might be mad at *me*."

"I'm not. I'm sorry I couldn't keep myself together, Quinn. Really sorry." Then, because maybe the moment felt too heavy for him, he pitched his voice into an impersonation of Yoda and added, "Miss you, I do."

It still made her smile. "I miss you, too." On this point, at least, she could be completely honest. She missed her brother—the talented, active, mischievous brother she remembered growing up with. Not the untrustworthy, manipulative stranger coke had turned him into. She definitely didn't miss dividing her time between her professional commitments and trying to keep tabs on him.

"That's actually part of the reason I called, besides to hear your voice. I wanted to invite you to come visit."

Her heart clutched a little. She leaned against the kitchen counter and noted a new goody basket on the island. Luke had cancelled this little hospitality, but either today was an exception or somebody new in housekeeping hadn't gotten the memo. "I will, soon, Callum. I promise."

"I'll be here all week," he quipped.

"I know. But it's going to be more like next month."

"Seriously? I mean, I know you're busy. I'm just…I'm fucking lonely, you know? You and me, we go way back."

It was an old joke, but she felt her lips lift anyway. "And we'll go way forward, too, but I can't get there right now."

"Are you on location for something?" His curiosity sounded a little forced. Their career trajectories were a sensitive issue. Because she wasn't on location, but rather facing down a setback of her own, she decided to level with him.

"Not exactly. I'm in my own form of rehab. Eddie sent me to fat camp at Paradise Bay for six weeks."

"No shit?"

"None whatsoever. I went into couch potato mode the last couple months." Callum didn't need to know why. He had no clue he'd sprained her knee when he'd accidentally tumbled them both to the sidewalk outside the treatment center. "The *Dirty Games* shooting schedule moved up, and now I'm under the gun to get in shape."

"Ah, man. We really are twins, aren't we? We go like Energizer Bunnies until we can't keep up the pace anymore, and then we crash, and end up sabotaging ourselves. We're our own worst enemies."

The observation sounded just enough like what Luke had said during their first session, it gave her pause. Callum didn't seem to notice, though. "Still, Paradise Bay. That's pretty sweet. Hey, I have an idea." His excitement shimmered over the line. "Why don't I get on a plane and complete the rest of my rehab there? We can keep each other company."

"Oh..." *No.* A sinking feeling settled in her stomach. "I don't think that's such a good plan."

"It's a *great* plan. They have a treatment program. Eddie suggested it at one point when he still handled me. I could stay with you. We'd be roommates again, and, you know, support each other."

Her stomach turned into a hollow pit. She couldn't be in charge of him again. Not now. There was too much at risk and she couldn't handle failing on all fronts. "Callum, there's a lot at stake here for both of us."

"For you, you mean," he argued, quick and defensive. "My stakes haven't changed in a long time, and we both know it, so at least have the balls to be honest. You think I'll fall off the wagon again, and I'll take you down with me."

"You want honesty? Here goes. I'm not a recovery counselor. I think I proved that last time around." Agitated, she dug into the goody basket. Before she questioned her intentions, she reached past the bananas, past the pineapple, to a renegade package of sugar-dusted polvorones that definitely didn't appear on the McLean-approved diet plan.

And clearly I have my own issues.

"Please, Quinn. Pleeeaaase. I don't think I can do this if you don't believe in me. Don't abandon me because you think it's easier to outsource my problems to someone else."

Like you've done, was the unspoken part of that accusation. Never mind that he'd broken every promise he'd made as a condition to moving in with her. Never mind that she'd "abandoned" him to the care of a top-tier treatment program and couldn't afford to keep him there if she forfeited the *Dirty Games* payday. Now, somehow, declining to do exactly what he wanted amounted to a vote of no confidence.

"How would you even get here?" She asked the question around a mouthful of cookie. "You can't travel on your own—nobody's going to be down for that—and I don't have the leeway to come get you." Even as she devoured another cookie, she tried to feed herself a dose of resignation. She already knew what was coming.

"Mom will do it."

Of course she would. Ann Sheridan came running whenever her son called. Callum was the shining star in their mother's eyes—her golden boy with the looks and talent to captivate everyone. Quinn's own early motive for participating in all the dance classes, drama workshops, and auditions had been a desire to win some notice. Luckily, she'd found performing satisfying in its own right, because it had never really worked as a way to claim any of their mom's attention,

"I can't—"

"Don't say no. Please." The ease with which he shifted modes from accusatory, to problem solving, to pleading left her off balance. As always. "I promise I'll be a Boy Scout the whole time. I'll make you proud of me again."

"Make me proud by finishing the program you're in. When you're done, and I'm finished shooting the movie, we can celebrate with a trip. Anywhere you want to go. You choose." She ate another cookie without tasting it, and dug into the bag for another. "It will be a good incentive for both of us." *What the fuck are you doing? Stop eating.*

"You're choosing a movie role over me." Mr. Accusatory returned with a vengeance.

"I can't, Callum. I just can't."

"You're there with a guy—"

"No." But there was some shameful grain of truth in his words. For the last five days, she'd toed the line with Luke, and felt like she'd forced him to rethink his opinion of her. She didn't want to expose this side of her life to his scrutiny.

"You're choosing *a guy* over your brother."

"For the last time, there is no guy."

"Yeah right. Enjoy Paradise, Quinn. Enjoy your fucking movie role, and this fucking guy, and your whole fucking life. Thanks for nothing."

Silence sounded in her ear. She blinked rapidly to ease the sting of salt in her eyes. Recovery was a messy journey, full of swinging moods. Any expert would tell her not to take Callum's words or actions to heart.

Easier said than done, unfortunately. She lifted another cookie to her mouth. Then she looked up to find Luke standing on the other side of the kitchen like a shadow in his black T-shirt and shorts, staring at her with narrowed eyes.

Oh shit.

"Good cookies?"

She swallowed quickly and crumpled the wrapper. "What cookies?"

"Wrong answer, Trouble. In the gym. Now."

Chapter Seven

Luke stalked toward the same open doors he'd entered through a minute ago when he'd been looking to track down his tardy client. She'd worked hard this morning, just like she had the entire week. He had no complaints about their momentum. Her conditioning was kicking in, and he planned to push her until they hit a wall, then back off and come at her from a different angle. He hadn't seen the wall on the horizon yet, but that was before he'd walked into her kitchen and found her sneaking cookies while on a personal call with some fucker. Some fucker she *missed*.

The knowledge simmered inside him, uncommonly volatile, and for the sake of his sanity, he chose to condense it down to, *No. Just no.* Then he mentally shoved the mess into a compartment, slapped a "Later" label on it, and closed the lid.

Sneaking sweets to get through a difficult personal moment, though? That was something to tackle now, as well as something to draw a line in the sand over. The habit undermined their chances of success, and, more importantly in the long run, wasn't an effective way to manage stress. He intended to put a stop to it, and he was prepared to use whatever method proved most effective.

He heard the patter of her cross-trainers against the cobblestone as she chased him across the courtyard.

"Wait. Luke...wait."

He continued into the gym, picked up his tablet and water, and turned to face her.

She held up her hands and offered him a disarming smile. "Look, I'm not going to make excuses—the kitchen didn't drop off my lunch."

Impeccable timing. Great delivery. He didn't return her smile. "Maybe you're not taking this seriously, but I *am*. I have a business to run, and I put a vacation on hold for this." His anger wasn't entirely manufactured, because everything he said was true, but he'd expected the cheating. Most clients deviated from the plan at some point—often early in the process when the food cravings hit hardest and the results of challenging workouts and a better diet weren't yet visible. "You're not willing to do what it takes to succeed."

"I am. I swear." She rushed to him and raised her hands to his chest, as if her paltry hundred and twenty-five pounds could prevent him from moving. "I just lost track of myself for a moment."

"I can't monitor you 24/7, Quinn. Nobody can, other than you, and if you're not up to the job, then we're both wasting our time. This won't work if I can't trust you."

"You *can* trust me. Please, Luke." She looked up at him with a rare show of genuine panic in her eyes. "Give me another chance. I promise I'm not wasting your time. Let me prove it."

This was exactly what he wanted from any client at this stage—the wavering stage—a renewed commitment to fight for the goal, and the determination to prove she could do it.

But for some perverse reason, with Quinn, he couldn't let it go at just words. "Prove it? How? Losing the role clearly isn't a sufficiently immediate and motivating consequence for you. What possible consequence can I impose that's more persuasive?"

Pink tinged her cheeks. She dropped her lashes, took a shuddery breath, and looked up at him again. "You'd have to…punish me."

No. No, this was going down the wrong path, and yet he felt the inevitability of it even as he tried to put on the brakes. Gently, he warned, "You couldn't handle it."

"Try me. Let me prove you wrong."

She licked her lips after she tossed out the suggestion. No. Not a suggestion. A dare, which was essentially a default setting for Quinn. He walked toward the door.

"Please."

Etched-in-stone rules faded like weathered hieroglyphics on an ancient ruin. The exquisitely fucked-up convergence of exactly what he shouldn't do, and exactly what she needed him to do twisted inside him, becoming a single, inescapable imperative. He closed the door and clicked the lock.

"Bend over the hyperextension bench and pull your shorts down."

Her breath hitched, but a glimmer of relief shone in her eyes. "You dirty pervert."

"Over the bench. Now. You've got five seconds."

Hands slapped the sides of her thighs as her eyes darted around the gym. "Which one is the hyperextension bench?"

He pointed. She marched to the angled apparatus, hooked her heels behind the crossbar, and leaned into the padded bench designed to support her hips. Then she draped herself over it and gripped the handholds while she squirmed around looking for the least demanding position. Finally she reached around and slid her tight, white shorts down to expose the top half of her ass.

He drew in a breath to clear his head. Get his bearings. "Lower." His voice sounded gruff to his own ears.

She made a compliant sound, and pushed the shorts down to bare her ass properly. He stepped up and ran a fingertip along the back of her knee brace—a reminder to both of them that she wasn't as invincible as she liked to project. "Comfortable?"

"Just ducky. Wake me when you're done."

"Don't worry. You'll be very awake by the time we're done." He brushed his fingers up her leg, along her hip, and brought them to rest at the base of her spine. "Head up."

All her muscles tightened as she obeyed.

"That's good. Now, tell me the rule, Quinn."

"W-what rule?" Her question revealed genuine confusion and only a little distress.

He placed his hand across the small of her back, reassuring. "The rule you broke. You know the one."

"I…um…" She shifted again, as if the air itself itched her bare skin. "I'm only to eat the prepared menu, unless you tell me otherwise?"

"Exactly. And did I tell you to eat the cookies?"

Her head drooped. "No."

"How many did you have?"

"Oh God. Three?"

He smoothed his hand over her back once more. "I think it was more like ten."

"Five!" Her head popped up again. "I ate five."

"Okay." He patted her once and then removed his hand. "You're going to count them off. Nice and loud. I want to hear each number clearly. Do you understand?"

She nodded.

"Respond verbally, please."

"Yes, dammit. I understand."

"Are you ready?"

Her body tensed. "Yes."

"All right. Let's get started." But then he waited another long moment. Waited until she dug her toes into the floor and pushed her hips up a barely perceptible degree. Not just consent. A request. Her low moan vibrated with anticipation.

He slapped his palm across one cheek…

"One," she cried, then added a surprised, "two," when he immediately backhanded the other unsuspecting cheek.

"*That's* one," he corrected, and watched a tinge of pink bloom across the smooth, pale skin. "Are you prepared for the rest of your punishment? Be sure of your answer, because I'm not going to stop and check in again."

"I…yes. I'm prepared."

He doled out the rest in rapid succession, giving her just enough time to draw in a breath after she called out each number. By the end, she was breathing heavy, her skin flushed with histamine-dilated blood vessels inflamed by the minor impact of his callused palm against her pampered ass. He was in a hell of his own making—a hell he'd entered as soon as he'd agreed to take her on. A hell that only got deeper and more damning the more time he spent with her. He wanted…

Unable to resist, he skimmed a fingertip low. She eased her thighs apart in what might have been a sneaky little move, except her body betrayed her. His head went light and his cock went heavier than humanly possible. If he accepted her subtle invitation, and instructed her to lift her hips, he'd find her hot and ready. But if he did that, right now, he wouldn't have the self-discipline to leave without taking a taste. And once he catered to that pussy, she'd have all the power and she'd know it. He'd be the next thing to useless in terms of motivating her to follow the program. Instead, he drew a figure eight along her tender skin. Goose bumps rose in the wake of his touch. "Relax. We're done with the preliminaries."

She parted her legs as far as the shorts would allow. "There's more?"

It took everything he had in him to keep some semblance of the higher goal in mind. The point was to break down her defenses and get to the true reason she undermined herself. "Yeah. Now we're going to have some cognitive therapy."

"Excuse me?"

"Time to talk."

"I don't need to talk." Her rebuttal was instant.

He traced the figure eight again. "You don't know what you need. That's how you ended up here."

"Fine." She let the word out in a long-suffering sigh before she wrapped her hands around the handles and started to push herself up.

He restrained her by cupping the back of her neck. "No. Stay there. I didn't tell you to move."

"Luke..." Her hands fluttered up for an instant, like restless wings. "I can't talk like this."

She sounded more than a little distressed, which told him she felt vulnerable now that the predictable punishment was over. And that's how he wanted her—vulnerable, unable to anticipate what came next, and less likely to muster up her typical countermeasures.

"That's unfortunate." Tempting his fraying control, he knelt and placed a whisper-soft kiss on a mark that hadn't quite faded. A spot where he suspected the sting still lingered. "I thought you could handle this, Trouble. Apparently we're just going through the motions." He straightened and backed away.

"Okay, okay. Wait." She lowered her head and wrapped her fingers around the handles, accepting his requirement. "What are we discussing?"

The compulsion to demand to know whom she'd been talking with hit him hard, but he banked it for two reasons. First, he wasn't sure she'd tell him, and she'd be within her rights not to, because certain areas of her life were private. Second, the thirst to know originated in an uncharted part of him—a jealous, territorial part of him he hadn't even known existed before he'd met her—but it sure as hell existed now. It didn't care about rules, and he feared giving in to it at all would be like putting out a fire with gasoline. He didn't need the information to get to the heart of her motives for cheating on her diet.

"Why did you break the rule?"

"I was hungry and distracted." She lifted her hands in a jerky, exasperated gesture. "I barely even realized I was eating, much less what I was putting in my mouth."

He came around to the front of the machine, crouched, and lifted her chin until their eyes met. Then he shook his head. "Uh-uh. You dug through all kinds of healthy options to get to those cookies. You sought them. Chose them. Try again."

"Luke..."

"Quinn."

She closed her eyes and took a deep breath. "I don't know. I was weak, and I thought I could get away with it. Satisfied?"

"Not at all. Look at me."

When she did, every ounce of her acute misery shined like unshed tears. She honestly didn't know. He steeled himself against her plea for him to tell her the answer, and continued. "We've got five weeks to figure it out."

"Can't wait."

Because he heard the exhausted relief behind her go-fuck-yourself bravado, he let it slide. He'd pushed her far enough for one day. Just to remind her he was on her side, he hiked her shorts up and snapped them into place, before making his way to the door. At the threshold he paused. "You don't like to show weakness to anybody. I get that. You prefer to handle your problems privately, on your own terms. I get that, too.

But your coping mechanisms flat-out suck."

Somehow, despite her position, she managed to roll a shoulder. "Add it to my list of flaws."

"It's not that simple. This particular flaw jeopardizes your goal, which makes it *my* problem. Luckily, I have a solution."

Her eyes narrowed. "You don't say?"

"I do. For the duration of our time together, Quinn, you don't have the privilege of exercising your own discretion. When you have a weak moment, you don't attempt to deal with it on your own. You tell *me*. When you need help, you ask *me*. Day or night. Got it?"

"Yes."

Her capitulation told him he'd wrung the fight out of her for today. He decided to press his luck. "Want to color in the rest of the picture about how you sprained your knee?"

"There's nothing to tell."

Nope. She still had some fight in her. But he didn't. "I think you do better with clear expectations, so let me make one more thing absolutely clear. I'm giving you my best, and I expect the same from you. Our contract requires you to follow the diet and exercise regimen I've designed to meet your goals. Anything less than full compliance and that deal isn't worth the paper it's written on. You're not just wasting our time, you're wasting your money, and we might as well cut our losses and call it quits. Take the rest of the afternoon to think that over." He sure as hell couldn't train her right now. He'd be spending the foreseeable future jacking off like his life depended on it. "I'll see you here at nine tomorrow."

• • •

Was praying for death a sin? It probably didn't matter, because prayers or not, she was going to die. Soon. Sweating like a pig, while sitting spread-eagled on a godforsaken torture machine. The only hope Quinn clung to was that she wouldn't beg for mercy first. With her eyes squeezed shut against the pain of that possibility, and the pain of her straining thigh muscles, she reinforced her hold on the grips by her sides and slowly pushed her knees together one more time…held for five seconds, and released…

The clang of the weights slamming back to their stack covered the sound of her groan. More or less.

"Keep your abductors engaged the entire time." A strict finger drew a triangle high along the inside of her thigh while Luke's cool voice issued instructions. "I don't want to hear weights bang. I expect you to stay in control as you return to the starting position. Ten more. Proper form this time."

Ten more? Oh God. She couldn't do it.

You have to. He didn't want to be there in the first place, *wouldn't* be there except for the fact that he owed Eddie the favor, but if she didn't hold up her end of their deal, would he call the contract void and leave?

She definitely couldn't let that happen. She needed him. She'd made progress, yes, but she wasn't in top form yet, and she definitely couldn't do this to herself. Which was why she'd been on her best behavior for the last two weeks—since he'd ordered her over a bench and doled out discipline so staggering, she still felt the aftershocks every time she thought about that afternoon. And she thought about it constantly. The real punishment hadn't been the spanking, or his tough words in the face of her failure. No, it had been the way he deftly drove her need into the red zone and then left her there, aching and unsatisfied.

The punishment continued, every second of the day, with every brush of his body against hers, every correction he made to the angle of her back, or the position of her hips, or even her breathing. She thought of him when she dressed, giving attention to whether he would approve of the clothes. She thought of him when she ate, knowing he'd chosen the food. She thought of him when she soaked in the bath at the end of the day, easing each sore muscle he'd worked to the limit with ruthless expertise, making her more aware of her own body than she'd ever been in her life. She dreamed of him when she slept, and in her dreams, he didn't walk away after spanking her. He stayed and did other things. Domineering things. Soothing things. Things that made her wake up sweaty and on the edge of an orgasm she never quite managed to capture. He'd reduced her to an agonized state she couldn't escape, and couldn't relieve.

Luke was in her head so deep, she worried she'd never get him out. Not just worried her, no, it scared her. Letting him get to her in such an unprecedented way was just plain dumb. At the end of this, they'd go their separate ways. Sooner, if she didn't walk the line to his satisfaction.

"Let's go," he said, cracking an invisible whip. Her skin tightened in response to his order.

She gathered her strength for another rep, appalled by the inelegant grunt the effort provoked, but the strain of pushing her knees together against the resistance of the weights quickly burned any shame away. Struggling through the rep, performing the exercise exactly as he specified, sent her into a whole new sphere of agony.

"Good. Perfect. Give me nine more just like that."

A glow of pride now accounted for some of the heat in her face. Okay, this struggle also gave her a whole new reality to confront. She wanted to meet his expectations not simply because she couldn't afford to lose the role, or because she refused to give him the satisfaction of defeating her, but because she wanted to earn his praise. She wanted to *please* him.

"Hey, you're not on a break. Knock these out. We've got other things to do today."

She wanted to *kill* him. No, death was too easy. She

wanted to torture him just like he was torturing her. Drawing on nothing but raw anger, she pumped out three more reps in rapid succession, but halfway through the fourth her muscles locked. She couldn't push her knees together, but she didn't have enough strength to let the weights down lightly, as he'd instructed. And if she didn't follow instructions, she'd hand him the excuse he was waiting for. So she froze there, breathing heavy, unable to continue but afraid to admit she couldn't.

"Do we have a problem?"

There was absolutely no compassion in his question. Only expectation. Expectation she had to meet, because falling short gave all his unfounded initial impressions of her the basis he needed to write her off as a lost cause.

Her legs quivered. "No," she lied. "I just need…" She bit her lip, because otherwise she really would beg.

"Look at me."

She forced her eyes open and focused on him. He knelt in front of the abductor machine, his inscrutable gaze leveled on her. His smoothly shaved cheeks weren't flushed from exertion. His finger-combed hair wasn't dripping with sweat. The sadistic bastard looked cool, and inexcusably handsome. She tried to hold on to the resentment, use it for strength, but a slippery panic was too all-encompassing to leave room for anything else.

"What do you need, Quinn?"

"Nothing. I—" Fuck it, her legs were going to give out. The weights were going to fall. She was going to lose.

"Six more," Luke prompted.

A combination of sweat and failure burned her eyes. Her vision blurred. "I—I can't." She coughed an oversize sob from her throat. "I *can't*."

"Uh-uh." His voice came from very nearby now. He'd leaned in close. "You don't say those words to me. Ever. What *do* you say?"

"I don't know. I don't." Screaming muscles erased her ability to think. Everything was breaking down—mind, will, body. All she could do was sit there, panting and trembling, as tears scalded her cheeks and her world condensed into waves of pain…from overtaxed muscles, from falling short. From being reduced to begging. "Please?"

She didn't think the situation could get any more unbearable, but then Luke's big hands settled between her legs. Long fingers grazed the abbreviated hem of her yoga shorts. A sudden bolt of need introduced new pain. Her breath hitched. Urgency gripped her, renewing her struggle to push her knees together so parts of her, ridiculously desperate for his touch, wouldn't be so susceptible.

"I appreciate the manners, but no. That's not it. Try again. What do you want from me right now?"

"Help?" Blind instinct pushed the word from her lips, and as it echoed around the room, some reinforcement inside her broke. She cried the word again—literally cried it—without the armor of a quick retort, or face-saving follow-up.

"Finally."

The next thing she knew, he took the burden of the weight from her. Slowly and carefully, he guided her thighs apart, releasing her agonized muscles from the device. Relief had her slumped against him, face pressed to his chest while a brewing cauldron of emotion she'd pushed to some back burner bubbled over in incoherent sobs.

Anger boiled hottest. Anger at Callum, for hurting himself, and then her. If she really wanted to, she could blame him for every aspect of her current predicament. But no, she reserved plenty of blame for herself. She should have called him out sooner—when he'd first started disappearing at odd hours, and cash started disappearing from her wallet—instead of floating along on the path of least resistance until it just wasn't possible anymore. Guilt brewed, too, for giving in to the urge to hide her suspicions and pretend everything was all right simply because she wanted it to be. Hope could be a dangerous thing, and disappointment tasted very bitter.

All the anger, disappointment, and bitterness tumbled out of her in a ragged, inarticulate torrent of desperation. "I'm sorry…I need help…please, don't leave."

Luke held her to him with one hand at the nape of her neck. The other made long, slow sweeps along her thigh. "Be still. I'm not going anywhere."

She was clinging to him. Clinging, and bawling, and drenching his shirt. Jesus, she hadn't broken down like this since…hopefully she'd *never* broken down like this, but now that the dam had burst, she couldn't seem to stop the tears. The realization created its own kind of panic, but maybe Luke picked up on it, because even as she stiffened, he tightened his hold and kept her in place.

His patience helped her get control of herself. Sort of. Her breaths still ended in pathetic little whimpers, but she started to notice other things—the solid cushion of his pec supporting her forehead, and the slow, steady drum of his heart. "You're looking for an excuse to leave." Even as she said the words, she snuggled into him, lifting her face to the underside of his jaw so she could inhale the scent of his aftershave.

His hand stilled on her leg. "I'm not leaving you, Trouble."

The genuine surprise in his voice sent her heart into a reckless little spin, until he added, "I made a commitment."

"To Eddie," she muttered, as disappointment shackled her chest.

"To you, Quinn." He tried to lift her chin, but she burrowed her face against his throat. "I made a commitment to you, and I'm not going to break it. Behave badly. Push all my buttons. Do your worst, because I can take it. There's no way I'm leaving."

Chapter Eight

Luke wasn't sure what possessed him to admit that out loud. He blamed the soft caress of her breath on his neck, the weight of her breasts against his chest as she rested her weary frame against him, and the little quiver in her thigh… just under his fingers. His body immediately reacted with an involuntary response of its own.

"You big bully," she said against his throat. Her voice was still watery, but there was no malice in it. "You let me think that if I didn't leap up the moment you said jump, you'd cancel the contract."

"I never said that." He ran a palm along the back of her head and down her hair. "I told you if you weren't prepared to follow my instructions, you were wasting your money and we might as well call it quits. *I'm* not going to quit on *you*, Trouble. I'm always going to do right by you, and I'm trying to make sure you do right by yourself."

It sounded proper, didn't it? Like the promise of an invested professional. Nothing in the words revealed the fucked-up truth—he was getting far too invested in her, and there was absolutely nothing professional about it. But just in case, he forced some exasperation into his voice and added, "It took me three damn weeks to wear your stubborn ass down. We're finally making real progress. There's no way I'm giving up on you now."

"So these past weeks, while I've been running, jumping, and training like a bitch, you've been setting me up to…what? Cry uncle?"

The indignant accusation helped bank his lust. Slightly. He smoothed his hand along her ponytail. "To know your limits, Trouble. I need to be able to trust you to tell me if you can't take anymore, and you need to trust me, too." Another spasm rippled through her tight abductor. He dug his thumb in and slowly circled. "Trust me to help you."

She moaned. The sound vibrated directly into his chest.

He swallowed and eased off the muscle a fraction, but circled again. "Does it hurt right here?"

"Everywhere. I hurt everywhere." Her confession fanned his collarbone, but he detected relief in her voice as her muscle relaxed.

"Huh. I thought I heard something."

"Me, complaining?"

"That, I'm so used to, I block it out," he teased. "I could have sworn it sounded like… No." He shook his head. "Couldn't be. I must have misheard."

"What?" She drew back and looked at him with huge, curious eyes.

He stared right back at her, not bothering to restrain the brow he felt lifting. "Are you asking for my help?"

Her response consisted of a quick hiss as another spasm tensed her thigh. "Ow. Ow…*Jesus!*" She clamped a hand to the pain point and groaned.

"Breathe," he said, and swatted her hand aside so he could squeeze the protesting muscle.

She sagged against him again, her exhale unsteady as she fought the cramp. Keeping the pressure on her thigh, he eased his free hand down to tend to her other leg, to prevent more spasms before they started. After a few moments spent concentrating on the sound of her labored breaths as he carefully worked the tight abductors, he slowly became aware of other things. Things like the small, needy moans coming from her throat, and the tangle of her fists in his T-shirt.

"Better?" He told himself to stop moving his hands over her thighs. "Or does it still hurt?" His question sounded inappropriately hopeful to his own ears.

"Hurts," she gasped and scooted closer, coming up against the constraints of the machine. "So bad."

"Where, exactly?" he countered, struggling to keep things clinical.

"Higher." She rubbed her upper body over his, like a cat.

"Quinn..." But his hands were already gliding higher, while his self-discipline slid away. He was losing this battle.

"Please, Luke. I've been hurting for weeks. It never lets up. It never goes away. You have no idea."

Oh, but he did. He knew the kind of pain she was talking about all too well, because he'd been living with it for weeks, too. Every time he let his mind off the leash, it wandered back to that moment when he'd had her draped over the hyperextension bench, bare-assed and breathless. Sometimes he imagined walking around the front, freeing his aching cock from his shorts and feeding it into her waiting mouth. He imagined her head bobbing, her body tensing and flexing as she drained him so thoroughly, he had to hold onto the pull-up bar overhead to keep from sinking to his knees. Other times, he stepped into position behind her, looped an arm around her waist, and thrust into her, balls deep, while she gripped the handles and arched up until he could watch her face in the mirror as she came.

But all of that was normal. Relatively. Just looking at her constituted a sex act, and he appreciated sex as much as any other man with a pulse. Yes, he wanted her, but like everyone else, he occasionally wanted things he couldn't have. Wanting her didn't trouble him. What troubled him was how much he looked forward to seeing her every morning, or how hard it had been, lately, to dismiss her at the end of each day and walk away.

That was not normal. That was dangerous, because she was a client. His role in her life was strictly temporary, and subject to limits. Hell, there was a guy at the other end of a phone with whom she traded phrases like, *I miss you, too…*

"Please," she repeated, her voice a broken whisper. "You told me to ask when I need help. Luke, I'm asking."

…and she could be manipulative as hell. Seducing him into breaking his own rules amounted to an attempt on her part to equalize the power in their relationship. He couldn't allow her to succeed, but recognizing her motivation didn't stop his hands from moving—didn't even make them pause. One scooted her hips forward, forcing her thighs wider. The other untangled her fist from his shirt.

A voice inside his head growled, *Fuck the guy at the other end of the phone. She's not with him right now. She's with you. She's not asking him for help. She's asking you.*

How much of that enlightened sentiment accounted for his motivation?

Doesn't matter. You've already walked a fine line with her once. You can do it again.

"I'm going to help you, Quinn."

His chest muffled her sigh. "Thank you," she murmured, and the gratitude rang sincere. He had to remind himself she played roles for a living.

But then she added, "I promise not to forget you don't like me," in a husky murmur that sounded a little too honest.

"I like you," he corrected, not bothering to mask the sincerity of his words as he wrapped his hand around her ponytail and eased her head back until their eyes met. "I like you so much, I'm going to help you help yourself."

"Help me…what…?" Her question hovered in the air like anticipation as he guided her hand between her legs and pressed it there. Uncertainty flashed in her eyes.

More theatrics, or did the idea of getting herself off while he watched actually trigger some self-consciousness? Either worked for him. "Help yourself."

Her lips firmed into a line—a tiny show of mutiny—before she shook her head. "That's not the kind of help I'm asking you for. You know what I want."

He didn't back off. She'd dragged them to this line, and by God, she was going to walk it. On his terms. "Oh no. I think you misunderstand how this works. You're permitted to ask for my help, but you don't get to specify my methods. You're not in charge here."

One blond brow lifted. "I was kind of hoping *you* would take charge," she argued, immediately shifting tactics. No wonder he hated leaving at the end of the day. It wasn't easy walking away from someone who entertained him at the same time she challenged him on every level.

"I already have. You just don't realize it yet."

Her chin came up. "Your authority has its limits, even if your opinion of yourself doesn't. Sorry, Luke. This isn't going to work for me."

"Close your eyes, Trouble."

She released an exaggerated breath and slowly lowered her lids, somehow turning it into a small act of rebellion.

He picked up the towel she'd slung over the back of the seat, folded it into a narrow length, and tied it over her eyes. Then he brought his mouth close to her ear. "You're beautiful."

He could shift gears, too.

She released another breath, slower this time. "You think that's all it takes? Blindfold me, stroke my ego, and I'll come in my panties?"

"I'm simply stating a fact. You have all this beauty at your disposal, to enjoy anytime you please. Do you ever?"

Her lips parted. Her cheeks went a delicate shade of pink. "Of course. Everyone does. Don't you?"

An honest response, if somewhat defensive. She needed him to give her an admission, too. "Yes. Want to know what I think about when I do it?"

Her lungs expanded as she drew in air, and the tight nipples forming peaks beneath her white workout top nearly touched his chest. His lips pursed from the need to draw one into his mouth.

"Yessss."

"I think about you."

"Spanking me?" she volunteered, so quickly he knew it had become one of her favorite scenarios.

"Sometimes. That's more of an opening act than a finale for me. Nice as it is, usually I want more than your pretty backside turned up for me. Once I'm done giving that ass much-needed attention, I imagine flipping you around and setting you in front of me, just like this."

"L-like this?"

"Uh-huh. Leave the towel alone," he admonished when she fingered the fabric. "Do as I say and I'll tell you what happens next."

"I'm all ears…"

"Good."

"…and no eyes," she added under her breath.

When had he become such a masochist? Through his shorts, he wrapped his hand around his jutting shaft. Just for a second. Just to relieve the crippling pressure. "You know that show you did? Where you bounced around in a cheerleading outfit?"

"*Pep Rally*?"

"Yeah. There's a scene where you make out with what's-his-face behind the bleachers. They shot it in shadows, but at one point, the camera picks up a flash of your tits."

She pressed her hand to her torso, and then slid it up to cup her breast. "They didn't show much. It's TV."

What's-his-face had gotten an eyeful, though. Was what's-his-face the guy at the other end of the phone? "They showed the swell of your right breast, from the side. They showed the whole profile in shadow, while that lucky son of a bitch put his hands all over you."

"Luke McLean, have you jacked off to my TV-14 topless scene?"

"A thousand times," he freely admitted, and gave himself a hard pull. Hard enough to lift his balls. Hard enough to feel a tingle in the soles of his feet. "But lately when I jack off, I fantasize about other things."

"What things?"

Your mouth. About pulling you close and staking a claim to that smart, reckless, distraction of a mouth.

His heart kicked up at the prospect, but kissing Quinn took this from proving a point to something else. Something neither of them could allow. Pushing her to the breaking point meant one of them needed to stay in control. She'd defaulted to seduction—a choice that no doubt usually got her whatever she wanted—and he had to remember what she really wanted right now wasn't him, but the upper hand. And a little relief. He'd give her relief, but he'd keep the upper hand.

"I think about having you here in front of me, pushing your top down so I can get a real look at you. Do that now."

If she hesitated at all, he didn't perceive it. True, she'd wanted him to cater to her needs, but she'd recognize he'd found another way of helping her. He didn't have to deny his attraction, only her demand that he act on it. *She* could act on it, secure in the knowledge that by abiding by his rules, she was actually seducing them both. Twisted, but effective. Apparently she agreed, because she flicked the skinny straps of her top off her shoulders, and then pushed the fabric down until her breast spilled over. Her low, shuddering sigh topped the moment like a cherry.

"I imagine you filling your hands with them. Lifting and kneading and showing me just how you like to be touched."

She was so suggestible, his words alone tightened her nipples, bringing the rosy crests to small, hard peaks. The air conditioner kicked on and cool air fell on them from a vent overhead. A little shiver and a throaty moan told him how hyperaware she was to every sensation. "Show me, Trouble. Show me what you like."

The room filled with the slide of soft skin against even softer skin. She stroked and squeezed silky smooth flesh, giving both breasts attention.

"You're rough with yourself," he growled, and gave himself another ruthless pull. She wasn't the only one who liked it rough.

"I have an imagination, too. You have big hands. I know how strong they are." The words puffed out as she captured one stiff nipple and dragged it through the tight clamp of her fingers. "I don't think you'd hold back on my account."

He watched, hypnotized, as her nipple turned deep red, just before springing free of the trap. "You might be surprised what kind of gentleness I'm capable of."

She frowned. Her hands stilled. "Not for me."

"Especially for you. Lower your hands."

She did as he asked, leaving herself as she was, with the wreckage of her workout top tangled below her breasts and the marks from her overeager obedience on her pale skin.

He shifted positions, putting his weight on his other knee, leaning in close enough to let his T-shirt graze her nipples.

"Oh," she gasped and jerked back so quickly, her breasts bounced against the awkward shelf of crumpled fabric.

"Yeah, I'd be gentle. Patient and gentle." He brought his face close to her breasts as he spoke, and watched his breath raise goose bumps on her skin.

She whimpered. He squeezed his eyes shut for a second to maintain control. "You'd be so attuned to my touch, even my stare would feel like too much."

"Oh God." She arched, blindly lifting toward his mouth. "Luke—"

"Is it too much?" For her, maybe. For him, definitely. He strangled his cock with his fist and cradled his throbbing balls in his other hand.

"It's too much"—she whipped her face left, then right, in a helpless search for relief—"but not enough."

"Then let me give you more. Put your hand in your shorts. Show me where it hurts."

The lack of artifice as she rushed to follow his command affected him more profoundly than a contrived, purposefully seductive move could. This wasn't Quinn the ice-cool actress. This was Quinn in need—shaky, desperate, unconcerned with winning their battle of wills.

"Here. It hurts here."

He lowered his head a fraction to watch her hand disappear under the cover of her little pink shorts. The move changed the angle of his breath over her skin, and she whimpered again. Her hand made a restless circuit between her thighs.

"Describe the pain." His was pounding, and constant. If he pushed his hips forward half an inch, the tip of his dick would touch her leg. Right about then it seemed like a half inch from heaven.

"There are two pains."

"Start with the worst."

"They're both unbearable."

"Quinn—"

"Okay. Okay." She lowered her chin to her chest and sucked in a breath through her nose. "Here…" Her knuckles stretched her shorts as she circled her fingertips around the top of her pussy. "I have a sharp, urgent pain right here."

"Rub it." His fingertips itched to do the job for her. He reaffirmed his grip on his shaft instead.

She shook her head. "No, no. I don't think I can stand to do that. It's too…sensitive. You do it."

"That's not the lesson." With all the willpower he could muster, he led his wayward pupil back to the task. "Help you help yourself, remember? Tell me about the other pain."

The tiny ridgeline of her knuckles subsided and she flattened her hand and shoved it lower. "It's deeper. More of an empty ache."

"Like hunger?"

"Uh-huh."

"You'll feel better if you fill it. Go ahead."

She rocked forward a little, angling her upper body and sending her unrestrained tits swinging perilously close to his face, and then let out an edgy moan as she achieved penetration.

For a moment he became so lightheaded, he worried he might pass out, but he blinked away the hazy fog because he refused to miss an instant of her pleasuring herself. "Better?"

"Oh yes."

"What helps most? Filling yourself, or massaging your clit with your palm?"

"They're both good. But I don't think it's enough." She shook her head. "Sometimes it's not."

He wasn't going to allow her to fail. "Are you using one

finger or two?"

"Just one. I'm so swollen—"

Christ. "Use two."

"I can't. Too tight."

"Two," he insisted, and pumped his cock, which suddenly struck him as monstrously huge. "At least two. Sink them in deep, and stir them around. Let me hear it."

Her breath hitched as she did what he asked. Her cheeks were as flushed and damp as they'd been when she'd strained against the machine, except now she strained for him. A few more seconds and he heard it—the slick sound of her body accommodating the slow, sliding play of her fingers.

"That's it. Keep going." Without really meaning to, he pumped his cock to the rhythm she set. Moments later, he was about to explode, but she was still stroking herself and grinding her hips with increasingly frustrated energy.

Finally, she slumped back against the seat, somehow managing to look both imperious and exhausted, with her chest heaving and her hand down her pants. "I can't. I told you I couldn't. I need *help*."

Damn, she was stubborn. "I told you not to say those words to me. Get your ass back up here and keep going."

"Not everything is meant to be a workout, you know." Despite the grumbling, she resumed her forward position, teasing him with the swing of her breasts. Breasts he'd confessed had the power to make him ruin his sheets while imaging his cock nestled between them. Molten heat rolled down his spine and pooled in his balls, a warning from his system about how well all this was working for him. The point of no return was fast approaching.

"If you do it right, it is."

"*This* is right?"

"Do you want my help, or not?"

"You sadist. Yes. I want your help."

He leaned in, too, and deliberately turned his face away at the last second so the side of his head brushed her breasts. He felt her nipple spear into his hair. His cock jumped in his fist.

Fast approaching.

"Oh God." She lunged forward, chasing the sensation, but the incline of the seat kept her from pitching herself into him.

"Who's in charge, Quinn?" His vocal cords felt thick and unwieldy. His whole body did, too, for that matter.

"You," she whispered.

He rewarded her by leaning in and turning the other way. She bolted upright this time, and her head fell back, exposing the graceful column of her throat. Her arm came up to cover her breasts in a gesture at once so protective and revealing, it nearly undid him. *Point of no return.*

No return.

"Who's in charge? Use my name."

"You're in charge, Luke. *Luke—*"

Her sudden inhale cut off the sound of his name, and then orgasm tore through her.

That did it. He groaned into his bicep and shuddered as three long weeks of unrelenting lust shot out of him in a white-hot fury.

Chapter Nine

"Damn, girl, you look like you just got it *good.* I don't even bat for your team, and I might have a long-distance orgasm from staring at all your afterglow."

Eddie's teasing smile and laughing eyes filled Quinn's phone. She automatically glanced up to the right corner of the screen, where her reflection stared back at her from a small square. Tousled hair. Flushed face. Shoulders bare to where the frame cut off, giving the impression she wore nothing but the dewy sheen of sex.

Yay, FaceTime. But oh, how she wished. Sadly, Luke hadn't given her anything to get sweaty over except workouts since last week when he'd "taught" her to help herself.

"Well, that would be one of us enjoying an orgasm, then. *I* just finished two grueling hours of circuits."

"Yeah, right. Why are you naked?"

"I'm not naked." She took a seat on the wooden bench just outside the glass-walled, open-roofed shower installed between the gym and the pool house, and adjusted the tilt of her phone so Eddie could see the fluffy white towel wrapped around her. "I've been set free for the day. I'm about to try the open-air shower." She lifted a brow. "Do you want to watch, or is there some other point to your call?"

"I'll skip the shower, thanks. I called to see how you're doing."

"Okay, I guess." A little pang of worry rippled through her.

"Uh-oh. What's wrong?"

"I don't know." Fidgety, she kicked her flip-flops off and squinted at her pedicure. It was on the tip of her tongue to ask him if he'd heard from Callum. She hadn't. Not a peep in the two weeks since she'd refused to bring him to Paradise Bay. But even if her brother had reached out to his former agent, Eddie wouldn't have taken the call. He stuck to a tough-love stance where Callum was concerned. No contact unless and until Callum demonstrated he'd cleaned up his act. If Eddie ever found out her brother had been so staggeringly out of his head he'd tumbled her to the ground and sprained her knee, she doubted he'd ever speak to Callum again. She moved on to a safer topic. "I'm working my ass off, Eddie, but for some reason, my ass isn't actually working off. I think I screwed up my metabolism or something."

"You look great. Seriously. I see the progress from here."

"Not enough. Luke did my midpoint measurements last week, and I haven't actually whittled many centimeters off the…um…problem areas."

"It doesn't work that way. A body doesn't shed fat in orderly increments."

"My weight actually went up a few pounds." She nearly whispered it, like a confession.

"Muscle weighs more. In the long run, though, your body spends more energy maintaining muscle. You'll hit a tipping point where you're not taking in enough daily calories to sustain it, and your metabolism will use any extra reserves you're packing for fuel. I bet at this week's assessment you're right where you need to be. Maybe even ahead of the goal."

She bobbed her head back in forth in a yada-yada-yada move, even though inside, she wasn't so calm. "Luke says the same thing, but what if I'm not?" What if she fell short? What if she lost the role, instead of the curves? Would Luke ever be able to see her as anything except a waste of his valuable time?

"If you're worried, talk to him. He's the best, as a trainer as well as a friend. You can trust him with anything—even things you choose not to tell me, for whatever reason." His inflection told her he knew there was something she'd held back.

She manufactured a sassy smile. "I'm not *worried.* I'm just wondering…is it too late for lipo?"

A clank of weights through the wall alerted her to the fact that somebody was working out in the gym. She eased a finger into the slat of the door, opened the shutters enough to peek through, and swallowed. Luke had stuck around after dismissing her, for once. He stood shirtless, with an array of muscles rippling as he brought two pulleys together in front of his chest, and then extended his arms and took them back out to his sides. Earbuds connected to the phone clipped to his hip ensured he couldn't hear her, but even so, she lowered the volume on her phone.

Eddie laughed. "It's about two decades too early for lipo. Trust the man's skills, Quinn. I can tell you he's pleased with everything you've accomplished so far."

"Really?" A pathetic part of her starving for his regard perked up. "You talked with him? When? What did he say?"

Eddie rolled his eyes. "You've been playing a high school student too long. You're starting to sound like one. He didn't pass me a note in biology, okay? He just said you were knuckling down and impressing the hell out of him, and…"

He hesitated, as if he thought better of sharing the next

detail.

"And *what*?" She pulled her gaze away from Luke doing an effortless flurry of pull-ups. "What did he say?"

"Nothing. Forget it. I've got to go."

"Eddieeeee."

"All right. Fine. Lord, save me from straight, white people." He held up two fingers to someone off screen—presumable his assistant—and then refocused on her. "I asked him if he forgave me for coercing him into taking you on. You know, fuck the I-owe-you crap, and whatnot."

Something painful expanded in her chest. Her breath. She was holding it, because the next words out of Eddie's mouth mattered more to her than oxygen. "What did he say?"

"He said yes."

A scramble of emotions made her eyes sting. Relief, euphoria, and something she didn't have a name for. Maybe Luke didn't resent her? Even as she pondered the question, her attention strayed to the gap between the slats. Beyond, the man capable of crushing her with a look, lifting her with a word, or driving her right out of her dirty little mind with his strict rules strapped on a pair of Everlast gloves and stepped up to the heavy bag suspended on a chain from the ceiling in one corner of the gym. His biceps bulged as he raised his fists to chin level and tucked his arms close to his body. Then he let loose with a lightning-fast, lethally powerful volley of straights and jabs. The smack of leather against leather sent a thrill down her spine.

"Earth to Quinn..."

She tore her attention away from her voyeur's view of Luke owning the shit out of the hundred-pound bag, and focused on Eddie. "What?"

Eddie's sharp green eyes narrowed. "I was going to say Lisa's about to email you an updated shooting schedule, but I sense I don't have your full attention. What do you keep looking at?"

Knowing a picture was worth a thousand words, she put her phone up to the slat to give Eddie a view of Luke in the gym, in all his shirtless, gleaming glory.

"Well, hell," he said when she turned the screen back to her. "Now *I* need a shower."

"Welcome to my world. Anything in particular I need to know about the updated schedule? I don't suppose I picked up a little more wiggle room?"

Eddie shook his head. "This schedule is a lot like your wardrobe. There is absolutely no wiggle room at all."

• • •

Jeeeezus!

The scream pierced through layers of guitar, drums, and a phantom-voiced thug singing about his heathen friends.

Quinn.

Luke shucked the boxing gloves on the fly, lost his phone while hurdling free weights he still needed to rack, and slammed through the flimsy door separating the gym from the alcove to the shower. His momentum sent the door crashing against the wall and ricocheting back toward him. He blocked with his shoulder as his eyes scoured the small space for Quinn.

He found her huddled at the far end of the shower, her body pressed up against the glass wall behind her like if she got close enough, she might magically pass through to the leafy haven beyond. A white towel barely covered the essentials, which made inspecting her for injuries a job he accomplished in a matter of seconds. No visible blood. No signs of a struggle. But blue eyes wide with shock locked on him as if she couldn't believe he stood there.

"What's wrong?"

She pressed a hand to her chest and let out a self-conscious laugh.

Before he could storm into the shower and shake her for scaring the crap out of him, or pull her into his arms and hold her until the adrenaline subsided—possibly both—she pointed to one corner of the vestibule, just inside the archway where he stood. "Sorry. He caught me by surprise."

He? Eyes trained on the corner, Luke stepped into the shower, and—

"Ugh. Jesus Christ. What the *hell* is that?" He had tile to his back before he even realized he'd retreated from the abomination of nature slung out along the cool porcelain. The blasted thing was the size of his forearm, but its dark scales blended into the gray tile.

"I don't know. Some kind of snake, maybe?"

"Uh-uh. It's not a snake. It has feet. A lizardly thing."

"Luke?"

"What?" He answered without looking at her. Bugs, he could handle. The part of Texas where he'd grown up boasted some whoppers. Same for spiders, rodents, bats, and birds. But he was not cool with reptiles. Yes, it was a phobia more than a legit fear, but logic didn't stop his heart from turning into a jackhammer in his chest. Caution dictated he keep all eyes on the footed snake.

"Why are you whispering?"

"I don't want to wake it."

"The eyes are open," she added.

Open, and unblinking. "Who says it has eyelids?"

"Good question. You're wearing shoes. Can you, like, kick it out of here?"

"Fuck no." He looked at her now. "Not unless you've got a universal antivenom stashed somewhere on your person."

She paled and her eyes darted back to the…thing. "Is it poisonous?"

"I don't know."

"Doesn't Mother Nature usually decorate poisonous species with bright colors?"

"I. Don't. Know." But spending the evening in a standoff with a potentially lethal lizard held zero appeal. Time to man up. He advanced to the center of the shower, and extended an arm to Quinn. "Come on. Walk behind me, and straight out the door. It's probably asleep."

She inched away from the wall. "You think?"

"I'm sure it's asleep." He waved her forward in a SEAL Team Six signal for move-your-ass, but as soon as she'd taken a full step, the animal skittered toward them. Quinn's shriek bounced off the walls, and the next thing he knew, he had a nearly naked woman climbing him like a jungle gym, and a surprisingly strong arm vised around his windpipe. He hefted her onto his back while retreating to the wall again. The bloodthirsty beast stopped about a foot away and stared God only knew where with its round, side-mounted eyes.

"Okay...okay. Quinn. Let me breathe."

The arm around his throat loosened a faction and he gulped oxygen. Over the rush of his pulse in his ears, he heard her say, "It's not asleep."

"Thanks, Princess Obvious. I got that."

"Jeez. It moves fast." She hoisted herself a little bit higher on his back. "Do you think it can jump?"

Shit. If there was a God listening to his prayers, no. "I doubt—"

That's as far as he got, because the ugly motherfucker charged them, and Quinn screamed again—way louder than he did—and scrambled to get a leg over his shoulder. He braced a hand on the wall to regain his balance, wrapped his other arm around as much of her as he could reach, and then he did what any guy in his shoes would do.

He ran.

Some idiot kept panting, "Watch your head…watch your head…" as he hauled ass out of the shower, the alcove, and the gym. By the time he reached the courtyard, a rational part of him recognized the need for speed had ended, but his fight-or-flight instinct didn't respond to reason. He kept on running, up the steps and through the open patio doors to her villa. Just inside, he slipped on a rug some interior designer had selected without regard for how easily a natural fiber turned into a hazard on ebonized floors. Gravity gave him just enough time to turn so he landed shoulder first, with Quinn tucked into the protection of his body.

The dull thud of impact was oddly comforting. No sharp pain, no scream from his passenger, no creepy clatter of tiny claws on polished hardwood. Just a diffuse ache that warned him he'd really feel it tomorrow. For now, he rolled onto his back, closed his eyes against the sunbeam slanting through the door, and gave his heart rate a moment to stabilize. The squirming, naked woman draped over him didn't help the effort, nor did the way her hands slid over his chest while her breathless voice repeated his name—although it reassured him she wasn't hurt.

"Luke. Are you okay? Say something. Speak to me."

"I'm fine." Not true. He was in trouble. Her towel was… he had no idea where. Hopefully nearby, but in the meantime, there was way too much naked skin pressed against naked skin. His hand, her ass. Her breasts, his chest. Their legs. A pair of boxer briefs and workout shorts wouldn't hide what all this was doing to him, and at some point soon, she'd dial in and realize she was a heartbeat away from finding herself pinned to the floor and fucked at a thousand miles per hour—for approximately three seconds.

As if to prove she didn't quite appreciate her predicament yet, she laughed. "I gotta say, I don't think I've ever seen anyone run that fast before."

He smiled, despite himself. "Are you insinuating my cat-like reflexes are less than heroic?"

"Perish the thought. I was duly impressed."

"Not half as impressed as me, at how you jumped on my shoulders in a single bound. Your Lena Xavier skills are strong."

Her chuckle tickled his jaw. "I probably didn't need to jump on you. I'm pretty sure your scream scared it to death."

"*My* scream? Please." He mustered up a disparaging grunt and pried his eyes open to see her smug smile. "*You* screamed. I issued a battle cry."

"Battle cry? Huh." She had the gall to crinkle her brows at him. "I could have sworn you just showed it the meaning of the word 'retreat.'"

"I saved the damsel in distress." He slapped her butt, and then immediately regretted it when his hard-on surged. "But hey, no worries. I can put you back out there with your friend, if that's your preference."

The swat turned her laugh into a snort. "Whoops. I'm bruising your fragile male ego, aren't I? Sorry. Let me try again." She batted her lashes at him. "My hero. How can I ever thank you?"

Then she leaned in, legs sliding to either side of his waist, and pressed a kiss to the underside of his jaw. Even though she only meant to play, he groaned.

Quinn's lips were as warm and soft as his darkest fantasies, and in those fantasies, they wandered everywhere. His cock jumped, eagerly volunteering to be her next stop, while at the same time he struggled not to pull her closer and capture those addictive lips with his own. Kiss them. Bite them. Coax them open and drink her in until she was all he could taste.

Her sudden stillness told him the moment she fully appreciated her predicament. And then, God help him, she trailed her mouth up and kissed his chin. Every nerve ending in his lips burned. He imagined fisting his hands in her hair and dragging her mouth the last few millimeters to his. Claiming it. Owning it. Violating it.

Control yourself.

His hands found their way along the line of her spine. "I accept—" He cleared his throat, because his voice stalled like a cold engine. "I accept your thanks."

She lifted her head and sent him a slow smile. "I'm not done thanking you, yet."

He clamped a hand at the back of her neck, under her hair, and traced her lips with his thumb. First the peaks and dips of the upper, and then the plump curve of the lower. "You're my client."

So get your fucking hands off her.

She saw a path straight through his mixed signals. "Not right now." Her tongue snuck out to lick the pad of his thumb. "I'm on my own time, remember?"

But she wasn't. Not really. During every second of their arrangement, she remained under his care, and while she didn't exactly embrace the fact, she'd finally stopped rebelling against it. This wasn't a power struggle, like their last few skirmishes. She'd worked her way through that phase, for now. But this was a phase, too, despite how real and potent the combination of attraction and affection might feel to her. And his feelings? His were so out of line, he refused to let himself go there. His personal feelings ultimately factored in not one iota, because the rules still applied. "Quinn, this isn't fair…"

That got through to her, though not the way he intended. She jerked back as if he'd slapped her. "Jesus, Luke. I'm not trying to buy you—"

"Not fair to *you*." He caught her wrists to hold her to him, because he needed to clarify. "You're here, thousands of miles from your normal support network..."

I miss you, too.

"...counting on me to help you accomplish something very important to you." Calling on every ounce of self-discipline he possessed, he levered them both up, and placed her on her feet. Then he found the towel she'd lost sometime during the tumble and tossed it over her like a cape. "This relationship is physical, and intimate. Everything about our respective roles makes you vulnerable. I'm controlling all your fundamentals right now, including what you eat, when you work, when you rest. That fosters a huge sense of reliance. Acting on that vulnerability isn't fair to you. It exploits your trust."

He couldn't judge by her expression whether she accepted his explanation. Unlikely, given she didn't see herself as needing anyone's protection, especially not from her own instincts. But she did, and the very fact that she required his services spoke volumes about that. It was past time for him and his unrepentant hard-on to get out, before he broke his own rules. He turned and walked toward the door.

Her voice stopped him at the threshold. "Maybe you should trust me to know my own mind?"

He shook his head and kept walking. "I know better."

Chapter Ten

Quinn couldn't bear to look, but she heard every tap as Luke entered her assessment results into the tracking app on his tablet. She pulled her spine straighter, because good posture made a girl leaner. Right?

His long, resigned sigh dropped an anchor of failure in her stomach. She opened her eyes and searched his face. "Are you kidding me?"

He gave her a grave look. "I am. Congratulations. You've earned a reward."

Shock paralyzed her vocal cords for a second. "Seriously? How much progress have I made?"

"All of our key measurements are down. Your overall BMI is down. Your strength and endurance are way up. Look at the definition you've got here"—he traced a finger along her biceps—"and here." The finger wandered down her torso, where she could see some actual abs now. "The better question is how do you feel?"

Horny would be her answer, especially if his fingertip wandered over any more of her body, but she cleared her throat and said, "Good. Energetic. Like if I can handle everything you've dished out over the past four weeks in here, I can handle an afternoon of takes on an action scene."

"Great." He walked to the little fridge and pulled a paper bag out of the small freezer section. "Do you want your reward here, or by the pool?"

By the pool sounded more relaxing. Her villa sounded even more relaxing, but he hadn't set foot in her domain for three days—since he'd treated her like a woman so screwed up she didn't know her own mind. He was clearly trying to enforce boundaries, and she was trying to let him because his rejection, no matter how well-intentioned, hurt like a bitch. But the notion of spending time with him somewhere besides the gym tempted her too much.

"Pool." She skipped out the door, into thick air, and dappled afternoon sunlight. "What's my reward?"

He strolled into the palm-shrouded courtyard at a more sedate pace. "Something from your list of favorites. Two things, actually. Have a seat." He pointed to the chaise lounges arranged side-by-side near the pool, with a small, wrought iron table between them.

She plopped down on one and watched as he placed the bag on the table. When she reached for it, he swatted her wrist. "Hands off, grabby. I have something to say before you dig in."

"Talk fast, Luke. I want my reward."

"Hmm. It's warm out here. Maybe I'll take a swim first." He sent her a mild smile, and then stripped off his shirt.

"Don't you dare—" His shirt landed in her face. She swept it aside, and prepared to toss it at him, but her mouth went dry at the wide planes of his chest, the hashtag of his abs, and the enticing line of dark hair trailing from below his navel to where it disappeared beneath the drawstring of his gray sweat shorts. Did he have anything on under them? One little tug and she could find out. As if he'd read her mind, a truly impressive muscle twitched beneath the gray sweats, and lifted in a gravity-defying show of strength.

She raised her eyes to find him staring down at her with his scowling, clench-jawed look. Forbidding was the word that sprang to mind, as if she needed a reminder that no matter what she did, or how much he wanted her, he'd never actually approve of her. Long-established defense mechanisms had her mustering up a smirk. "I thought you said my reward was in the bag?"

To her surprise, the comment earned her a laugh, and she realized some of his scowl had been self-directed. "I would leave the choice to you, but I don't really have any hope of competing with what's in the bag." He lowered himself to the other chaise, his big frame dominating the space, legs parted to accommodate hers, the insides of his knees almost brushing the outsides of hers.

Like a poorly trained puppy, her attention rambled over the thickly braided muscles lining his thighs and honed in on the barrier of loose, gray cotton splayed for her gaze, thanks to his manspreading. Was it a trick of the light, or did she detect—her vision narrowed and salt filled her mouth—sweat-dampened fabric? He'd said he was warm. Her tongue crept to the front of her mouth as she imagined freeing his balls from the shorts and cooling them down with her tongue.

The sound of Luke clearing his throat had her fixing her gaze on his face. His expression was entirely too knowing. "Before I lose your attention entirely, I want to tell you I'm proud of you."

Proud? She snapped her head up so fast, she nearly bit her tongue. "You are?"

"Yeah. This is not an easy process. Getting results requires physical and mental discipline, and frankly, not everyone can follow through. But you can." Clear hazel eyes leveled on her, and he added, "I am very proud of how hard you've worked."

A lump in her throat threatened to choke her. This was no doubt part of the program—establish need, assert control, dismantle resistance, and then slowly build confidence—but even so, his praise felt like rain after a thousand-year drought. To talk herself down before she did something stupid like burst into tears, she nudged his knee with hers. "You sound so surprised. Didn't think I had it in me, did you?"

He nudged her right back. "I knew you had it in you. Eddie wouldn't have called me for a client who didn't have it in her."

"Oh." The overwhelmed feeling subsided a bit. "Well, that's really more your faith in Eddie's judgment."

"Eddie's a smart guy. I respect his opinion, but once I reviewed the show, I agreed. Talent counts for something, but you're too good at what you do to be the kind of person who lacks commitment and follow-through."

Emotion threatened to swamp her again. She put everything she had into her work, but she didn't expect him to realize—or care. The compliment stunned her. She needed to find some perspective, because being *this* susceptible to his opinion left her feeling way too fragile. "You only watched the show to check out my tits."

He stared at her for a long moment, and then lifted a corner of his mouth up in the subtlest of smiles. Tension slipped from her shoulders. He was going to let her get away with diverting the conversation.

"Every job has perks."

"Speaking of which, do I get mine now?"

His smile went up a notch. He reached into the bag, drew out something about the size of an espresso, and presented it to her with a flourish.

Sweet Jesus, she really *was* going to cry. With shaking

hands she reached out and touched the mini-cup of imported Belgian chocolate ice cream. "For me?"

"All yours. I've got another one in the bag for me."

"Oh...come to mama." She swiped the treat out of his hand before he could change his mind, and tore the small, wooden spoon from the side of the carton. An instant later the sweet, cold magic of dark chocolate and heavy cream melted on her tongue. She didn't bother stifling her moan, but quickly scooped up another spoonful.

"You're going to give yourself brain freeze."

"I'm going to give myself an orgasm. Don't ruin it for me. I'm almost there."

He laughed and popped the lid off his. "Enjoy your reward, Quinn. You've earned it."

She did. Every ounce of it, in about five seconds. All too soon, she was scraping the bottom of the container, and silently sighing. Ice cream orgasms—so good, but so fleeting. She looked over at Luke.

He was in the process of bringing a spoonful to his mouth. A big spoonful. As he parted his lips, he caught her looking. His eyes narrowed.

"No."

Feeling playful, she batted her eyelashes at him. "Oh, come on. Sharing is caring."

"No way. I've earned a reward, too, and this is mine... hey—"

He jerked back as she landed beside him on the chaise, and then sucked in a breath and dropped his gaze. "Aw. See what you made me do?"

Following his line of vision, she looked down at his bare chest, where his spoonful of ice cream now left a chocolate trail down the vertical gulley genetics and discipline had chiseled between his pecs. Without stopping to question the wisdom of the impulse, she lowered her head and licked it into her mouth.

A low groan rumbled from beneath her lips, alerting her to the fact that she was running her tongue over smooth skin at the same moment the hot taste of testosterone cut through the sweetness of the ice cream. A tingling sensation started at her lips and traveled to far-flung destinations like shockwaves from an epicenter. Slowly, she lifted her head.

• • •

Blue eyes burned into him like flames. He couldn't look away, couldn't swallow. Could barely breathe. Her lips moved, possibly forming his name, but no sound reached his ears except the harsh imperative of his own inner voice.

Quinn…

Slender fingers closed around the hand he still held suspended between them, the small carton of ice cream still locked in his fist. His wrist turned like a doorknob under the slight twist of hers, and then something cold and sticky drizzled along his abs.

Don't…

Surely he'd said it out loud? Any other client, and he would have put a stop to this instantly, but Quinn blurred all the lines. She bent all his rules, and instead of finding it infuriating, he couldn't wait to see how she'd test him next. But accomplishing what he'd been hired to accomplish meant knowing how to push back when she tested the limits—keeping her focused and motivated, not succumbing to her attempts at distraction. Over the last four weeks they'd reached a level of cooperation that was working for her, and letting her have her way with him would complicate their relationship, and risk disrupting the hard-won momentum.

Don't…

Her gaze darted down. She licked her lips and lowered

her head. Her mouth touched his skin—cool and hot at the same time—and her tongue slid down his stomach.

Don't stop…

Oh yeah. That's what he'd said. His free hand tangled in her hair, his fingers sinking into the silky mass. Not to pull her away, but to guide her lower. Still clinging to his wrist, she hooked her other hand into the front of his sweats and slowly eased herself down until she knelt on the cobblestone between his parted legs.

That mouth. That mouth he couldn't stop thinking about glided lower, and his cock strained to meet it. She raised her head. He didn't remember abandoning his hold on her, but suddenly their fingers were tangling on the drawstring to his sweats. He shoved the shorts out of his way, or she did—he wasn't sure who deserved the credit—but the move trapped the head of his cock in the process, dragging it down until the drawstring gave way. His dick slapped his abs with a solid *thwack*, and he felt a moment of pride at her quick intake of breath.

And *fuck*…it was his turn to suck in his breath, because she took the ice cream from him, tipped the cup and dribbled two of her favorite things all over his pride. For half a second, they both admired her handiwork, then she placed the container on the table and whispered, "Ooops."

Every tether in his mind holding on to reasons why they couldn't do this snapped. "Somebody better clean that up."

She braced her hands on his thighs, lowered her head, and licked him from base to tip.

Not a prayer. He didn't have a prayer. He'd pictured her like this too many times. Dreamed of pushing into her lush mouth and staying right there until she finished him off. Groaning his surrender, he sank both hands into her hair and held it back so he could maintain the view. "You overlooked a few spots."

She licked him again, swirling her tongue as she went, teasing it over the very tip. "Mmm. This could take a while." Her lips brushed his crown as she spoke.

This could take another minute, tops. "Quinn..."

"I'm afraid I'm going to have to use my whole mouth."

Despite knowing full well what she intended to do to him, watching her slick her tongue over her lips in preparation, he still nearly thrust deep when she closed her mouth around him. The ungentlemanly instinct warred with his desire to see his cock slowly slide into the haven of her tightly sealed lips.

The slow slide won out, because apparently he did still possess a modicum of impulse control—maybe only enough to keep from artlessly fucking her mouth—but at the moment, it amounted to a major act of self-restraint. He held onto it while she worked her way up and down his length in an agonizingly leisurely pace. He held on to it when she abandoned his throbbing cock with a suddenness that wrenched a curse from his throat, and angled her head until her tongue laved his balls.

He tightened his fingers in her hair. "Christ, Quinn."

"It got everywhere," she murmured. "I want to do a thorough job." Planting a hand at the center of his chest, she pushed until he leaned back on his elbows, and proceeded to use a devastating combination of lips and tongue to chase down every possible drop.

He looked down the length of his body. Her hand smoothed his torso, stopping just shy of the place where his cock jutted like a sundial, and then stroked up along the same route, as if she couldn't get enough of his clenched abs. He tightened them for her, wanting her to feel every ridge.

Her forehead teased another hard ridge, nudging the back of his shaft each time she moved her mouth—and she moved it constantly. She wasn't ignoring a damn thing.

Her tongue took an unexpected foray, and his breath exploded from his lungs.

"Jesus. That's pretty fucking thorough."

She spent another few seconds showing him just how thorough she could be, and reduced him to threats, because it was threaten or beg. He sat up, speared a hand in her hair, and eased her head back until he could look at her. "If you don't stop right now, you're going to have another mess to clean up."

Bold eyes stared back at him, gleaming with challenge. "What would you make a mess of, Luke?" She smoothed a hand over her cleavage. "My breasts?"

Her hand was on the move before he could answer. She ran her palm up the back of her neck, dislodged her ponytail holder, and then combed her fingers through the long, silky cascade. "My hair?"

She swept it back, tipped her chin higher, and tempted him with lowered lashes. "My face? Would you like to come on my f—?"

"Your mouth." He manhandled his cock until the head hovered close to her lips. "I would make a mess of your dirty little mouth." It wasn't lost on him that she hadn't offered that option, though. A little ice cream only went so far, and it could be she didn't consider that particular type of mess much of a treat. "But I'd give you fair warning." He glided the tip of his cock over her lips, making them glisten.

"Who's going to give *you* fair warning?"

Not her. She dipped her head and took him throat deep. Reflexes she used to swallow went to work and he lost the ability to think. Her fingernails dug into his thighs and he didn't give a shit. She drew him in a little deeper, gave up a mere fraction of an inch, and then did it again. Down. Up. Up. Down. Bobbing her head in his lap in an unpredictable rhythm that pressed his balls against the cushion and never let him get in front of the sensations she pumped out of him.

He cupped the back of her head, allowed himself one fast, hard thrust before releasing her. "Fair warning," he managed to say through clenched teeth.

She kept right on going.

"I mean it, Quinn. If you don't want to take it in your mouth, you better stop."

She stopped moving, but left him lodged deep.

Sheridan smartassery at its finest. Because he wasn't certain she appreciated just how worked up she'd gotten him, he offered a final, final warning. "I'm three, maybe four seconds from coming like a motherfucker. My balls are so full, they ache. My cock feels heavy enough to anchor the Titanic. If you're not prepared to swallow fast and often, you need to get up now. Put me between your tits, your thighs… bend over and offer up your ass. But make no mistake Quinn. I'm coming, and I'm coming hard."

And then, God help her, she sucked all the slack out of her lips. He remembered bending forward. Vaguely registered grinding his forehead to the crown of her skull. From universes away, he heard a triumphant sound.

Hers.

A long, grateful groan.

His.

He stayed like that, hunched protectively over her, while she swallowed, and swallowed, and then cradled his wrung-out dick in her mouth, toying with him just enough to keep him semi-hard.

No good. He refused to let his tired cock languish there. She deserved only his best. Holding her shoulders, he pulled himself from between her lips. He slid free with an audible pop.

She curved her lips and raised her beautiful face to his. She glowed—a woman flushed with the power of bringing her target to his knees, and not yet overly concerned about the wisdom of her actions.

The next words had to come from him, and he needed to choose them very carefully. Something to put them back on solid ground, and reestablish their roles, despite the fact that she'd just owned him in a fundamental way.

With a barely perceptible move, she shifted her weight to her left leg.

The need for answers overrode caution—or maybe he simply wanted to push her boundaries as payback for letting her run right over his. "Tell me how you sprained your knee, Trouble."

The glow of triumph dimmed from her face, and her expression shuttered.

Yeah, wrong call. Pushing this particular boundary only made her close up.

I miss you, too…

She swiped her index finger to one corner of her mouth, then the other. Then she got to her feet. "Thank you for my reward."

"Quinn…"

She walked into her villa and closed the door behind her.

Holy shit, he'd fucked this up. Badly, and on every level. Crossed the line with a client, and then driven her away in a clumsy attempt to resolve jealousy he had no right to feel. And while all that was damning enough, it wasn't the worst of his transgressions. Not even close.

He sank his fingers into his hair and pulled until his scalp sang. She was a client. An actress. A bundle of reckless impulses wrapped in a package so stunning, it qualified as a defense mechanism.

And he was falling for her.

Fuck.

Chapter Eleven

The lovers strolling arm-and-arm along the shoreline in the distance up ahead probably thought the full moon hanging low in the star-strewn sky looked romantic, but to Quinn's tortured conscience, it looked like a judge surrounded by a jury of stars, aiming a big, accusatory eye directly at her. One she couldn't evade, no matter how many miles she logged trying to outrun her humiliation over the encounter with Luke that afternoon.

She focused on the couple. As she watched, the guy turned to the woman, pulled her into a kiss and…whoa… okay, in addition to finding a moonlit beach romantic, they also clearly thought they had it to themselves. Rather than thunder past and hurl an ill-tempered "Get a room!" at them, she changed direction and jogged back the way she'd come. After all, some people came to Paradise Bay for pleasure.

Not Luke. He's here as a favor to Eddie. He's here to do a job. He's told you this more than once, and still you…what? Put his dick in your mouth and hope an unrequested blowjob changes his mind?

He didn't stop you, a self-defensive voice inside her pointed out. *What about the spanking? What about the 'Help me help you'? He's no altar boy, either.*

True. But instead of giving rise to righteous indignation, the realization only made her feel worse—or maybe the pinch in her side from overexertion deserved the credit? Either way, she knew damn well she owned most of the blame for those incidents.

Why did she keep taking them there?

At first, admittedly, she'd done it as a pathetic attempt to gain a measure of control over him. He had a ridiculous amount of control over her, didn't particularly approve of her, and he'd been a real jackass about it initially. She hadn't been above trying to gain a little power by making him want her.

She dug her fingers into her side to ease the uncomfortable pressure, and acknowledged the motive possibly made her exactly the neurotic, narcissistic actress Luke had accused her of being during the call in Eddie's office. But things had changed since those early weeks. Power and leverage hadn't factored into her actions this afternoon. That had been nothing but genuine desire, and affection, and…something deeper. Something that just kept on getting deeper, no matter how much she wished it wouldn't, because he wasn't a jackass, as it turned out. He was a good guy—the kind of guy who paid a debt to a friend even when it went above and beyond the call of friendship, the kind of man who kept his promises to her even when she didn't necessarily keep up her end of the deal. A man who wanted her, but didn't *want* to want her.

Dammit.

She slowed to a walk before the pressure in her side escalated to a full-blown stitch, and tipped her head back to draw in slow, deep breaths. The moon glared down at her in silent recrimination.

You owe him an apology.

She bent over and rested her hands on her knees, swallowing the truth with a lungful of oxygen. In the morning. She'd apologize first thing in the morning. After that, she'd keep herself in line, and respect his rules, because he was a good guy. No matter how much she wished for more from him, he'd been very clear about what he was there to do…and what he wasn't there to do, and—

"You okay, Trouble?"

She was so busy making promises to get the moon off her back, she almost screamed when Luke called to her. She whipped her head up, but it took her a moment to spot him sitting a few yards up on the sand, staring at the ocean. Well, staring at *her* now that she'd moved into his line of sight, but originally staring at the water. The sight of him there, alone, made her realize she wasn't the only one miles from home, away from everything familiar, enduring six weeks of relative seclusion. She really didn't know how he spent his downtime—other than not with her—but by himself on the beach after dark hadn't entered her mind. It seemed broody, and lonely, and uncharacteristic, despite his self-contained nature.

Then again, she'd just taken a midnight run to clear her head, so it could be he hadn't cornered the market on broody, lonely, uncharacteristic behavior.

"I'm fine," she answered before the silence stretched too long, and made her way up the slight slope to close the distance between them. Her plan might have been to apologize first thing in the morning, but apparently the universe felt she ought to get it done tonight. As she approached, the moonlight glinted off something sitting in the sand beside him. A bottle. She narrowed her eyes to make out the label. Old Harbor Visitante 212, she read, and then shifted her attention back to him. "Are you out here by yourself…drinking?"

Correction. He definitely won the prize for broody,

lonely, uncharacteristic behavior.

"Nope." He upended the bottle to demonstrate it was empty, and then went back to staring at the waves.

She took a seat beside him in the sand, settling close enough to catch a whiff of roasted malt, dark chocolate, and a sting of rum. "Sending out a message in a bottle? Does it say, 'Please rescue me from my crazy client?'"

His lips curved up at one corner. "No. It says…" He let out a long, tired breath, and turned to her. His windblown hair and slow-to-focus eyes told her the bottle in his hand wasn't his first of the evening. "It says, 'I'm sorry—'"

"That's my line." Yes, it was rude to interrupt, but she really didn't think she could withstand an apology from him. *Sorry I didn't stop you from making a fool of yourself? Sorry I ever took this job? Sorry, but…*

"I never should have let that happen," he finished.

Wow. That was even worse than anything she'd come up with. Swallowing the rest of her pride, she forced a highly unconvincing laugh. "Oh please. Don't even. I jumped you."

Now he laughed, and then made her breath hitch when he cupped her cheek in his palm. "I'm bigger, taller, and strong. Trust me, Trouble, you did not jump me." His expression sobered and his eyes scanned her face while his thumb traced her cheekbone gently. It hurt how much she wanted to read into the absent gesture. "Trust me," he repeated, but this time his smile took on an ironic tilt, before he shook his head, and dropped his hand. "Right. Mr. Trustworthy. Believe it or not, I'm trying to do the right thing here. I'm trying to be fair to you." He blew out a frustrated breath. "And to me."

God, was she an idiot? "I know. I'm…." *Sorry.* She meant to say "sorry," but shame clogged her throat. Early on, he'd told her sex wasn't part of the services, because he wasn't some high-priced gigolo disguised as a trainer. Pride had forced her to assure him she wasn't a woman who needed to pay for sex, and then she'd completely dismissed that particular concern. Like it didn't apply, because she had feelings for him, dammit. But what about him?

Her motives came straight from her heart, but if she told him that, he wouldn't believe her. No, he'd already written off her feelings as an apparently commonplace byproduct of the highly physical and intimate nature of their relationship, and misplaced reliance on her part, or an inability to separate needing his help from plain old needing him. Maybe if he hadn't already spent some chunk of this evening trying to drown out the memory of crossing lines with her this afternoon, she would have taken another run at that wall. What did pride matter at this point?

But he *was* out here, using local cerveza to wash down guilt, regret…hell…probably a decent dose of plain old pissed-off, and if she couldn't read that for what it was—a big, neon warning sign that she was living up to the nickname he'd given her—then she really was an idiot. "I'm sorry," she managed to whisper, getting her voice behind the words this time.

"Don't." He turned to her again, and shook his head. "I have a lot of experience doing what I do. I know what's right, and I know what's wrong. I like to think I can handle anything at this point, but"—he reached out and traced her lips with a fingertip—"I'm finding it hard to handle you. I'm only human, Quinn." He sighed and stopped touching her. "And you're so damn…"

So damn neurotic? Narcissistic? Slutty? No way could she let him finish *that* sentence, even if she deserved every word of it. "Yeah. I'm hard to handle." She dredged up her shatterproof smile. "You're not the first person to think it. You won't be the last." Now she put a hand on his cheek, because his eyelids drooped and he seemed to be having a hard time focusing. "Driving people to drink is my secret, hidden talent."

His eyelids snapped up and he looked straight at her. "You don't have the first clue what your talents are, Trouble." He rested his forehead against hers. "Besides, I only had two. I just don't do it very often. It's counterproductive, and"—he broke off and yawned, hugely, then gave her a lopsided smile—"a shitty coping mechanism."

Her heart contracted a little at the sloppy grin. She eased back and combed his hair off his forehead with her fingers. "How about rest? How's that for a coping mechanism?"

He leaned into her touch for a moment, a low noise rumbling in his chest like the purr of a jungle cat when she raked her nails lightly over his scalp, but then he caught himself. The growl bottomed out into a groan, and he flopped down in the sand with his arm folded behind his neck. "Rest is prob'ly a good idea."

She raised her brows at him, but it was a wasted effort because he'd already closed his eyes. "I was thinking you should get some rest in a bed, maybe in your room?"

He lifted his other hand and gave her a thumbs up. "Give me a sec and I'll walk you back to your villa first." Then, without opening his eyes, he patted his chest. "Have you seen the sky tonight? Huge moon."

Yeah. Right about now, that big old moon was mocking her, but she couldn't resist Luke McLean, all tipsy and tired and splayed out on the sand in a navy blue T-shirt and rolled at the ankle khakis. She arranged herself alongside him and settled her head into the dip between his chest and his shoulder. The cloud-soft cotton under her cheek covered warm, vital muscle, neither of which muffled the slow, steady thud of his heart. Hers slipped another inch into the danger zone when a warm hand covered the one she'd rested on the center of his chest and then long fingers threaded through hers.

She looked at the endless expanse of sky, listened to the ancient lullaby of the surf foaming out against the sand, and the thunder of his heartbeat in her ear. After a moment, she whispered, "Luke?"

No answer. She lifted her head, intending to wake him, but just then, a light shot across the heavens in a glowing arc. A falling star. They were supposed to be lucky, weren't they? She strained her eyes to keep it in sight while she scrambled around in her brain for a quick wish.

Callum clean and sober.

No. That needed to be Callum's wish. She couldn't make it happen.

Okay, keeping the role.

Work? Really? When confronted with the power and magic of the cosmos, she'd waste a wish on something largely within her control?

Come on, Quinn. You know what you really want. Wish for...

Inevitably, she blinked. The streak of light disappeared before she could finish the thought, leaving her to wonder if something so rare and special had ever been intended for her at all.

• • •

Luke emerged from a ridiculously good dream of Quinn snuggled against him, with her soft breath caressing his throat and her hand tucked inside the waist of his pants, to a waking nightmare of Quinn snuggled against him, her soft breath caressing his throat and her hand tucked inside the waist of his pants.

And a hard ridge behind his zipper angling to meet it. Strangling a groan, he shifted until her hand fell away, and used his own to shove his relentless cock back into his underwear. Quinn mumbled something that sounded a lot like, "Gotta wish quicker," and burrowed her face into the curve of his neck.

No doubt. Or sleep deeper. Or best plan of all, not consume fifty ounces of beer before nodding off so he didn't wake up in the middle of the night with a bladder the size of Delaware.

At least that situation was easily solved, as opposed to the one presented by the woman cuddled against him, breathing in a slow, even rhythm that signified she'd slipped effortlessly back into dreamland. It figured Quinn slept with the same abandon with which she did most everything else. He carefully settled her on the sand and went to deal with Delaware.

Standing at the water's edge communing with nature, with no one to answer to except the ocean, the sky, and the salty air, he confronted the truths he'd hoped to evade last night with the help of barrel-aged stout.

First truth? He was here to do a job. Eddie and Quinn were relying on him to transform her into convincing action-hero form safely, and he intended to do it.

Another truth? Quinn was a beautiful, complicated, fascinating woman, and against his best intentions, he'd developed feelings for her. Strong feelings. Strong enough to warn him he wasn't getting out of this unscathed, and worse, a reckless part of him didn't care.

That said, getting personally involved with a client broke certain fundamental rules he'd learned the hard way a long time ago. It turned him into someone he didn't want to be—someone he'd have a hard time respecting—even though he wasn't a twenty-two-year-old up-and-comer anymore, and Quinn wasn't a self-absorbed diva prone to treat him like an accessory she'd bought and paid for. The fact of the matter was, for the term of their contract, he worked for her. In a town as small and thirsty for gossip as Hollywood, others *would* say it, and the clichéd whispers were hard for people to ignore. Particularly people like his employees, or the network of doctors and other health providers who referred clients to him, and staked their reputations to his by association, or his existing and potential clients, who might stop to question his professionalism.

So, no, as long as the contract remained in effect, he had to keep a lock on his emotions and behave like the fucking professional he was. Luckily, this issue resolved itself in two lousy weeks. Surely he could hold his shit together that long?

And afterward?

Well, hell. Who the fuck knew if there would be an afterward? Irritated, he tugged his zipper up and dragged his sorry ass back up the beach to where Quinn slept. He couldn't forget there was some petulant motherfucker on the end of a phone line whom she missed. She didn't want to talk about him, and insisted she wasn't involved with anyone, but she still took his calls. She still talked *to* him, which meant whatever they'd had wasn't over.

Maybe that was for the best, because his track record with actresses wasn't stellar, and time had only eroded his tolerance for the petty dramas of the Hollywood game. From his pocket, he dug out the card key that got him into the gym every morning. He palmed it, then bent and slid one arm under Quinn's knees, worked the other under her shoulders, and lifted her smoothly to his chest.

"Yes," she murmured as he got to his feet with her cradled in his arms. A quick glance down confirmed she still slept. Yes to whom? Yes to what? A hot spear of jealousy gouged a jagged path through his gut, but the burn subsided somewhat when she curled into him and exhaled his name in a dream-laced voice brimming with desire.

Parts of him responded immediately to her husky,

completely unconscious invitation. He carried her up the walkway toward her villa and tried to keep his hormones in sync with reality. Quinn thought she wanted him, but hey, he was also pretty much the only man in her world right now, not to mention someone she needed to help her attain something she desperately desired. He basically had her confined to a cage—a gilded one, but still, the fact that he was currently letting himself into her villa with his access key only underscored the point. And accepting more from her than trust in his expertise without giving her a chance to view their relationship from a vantage point free and clear of the current dynamic amounted to an abuse of that authority. Completing the contract didn't magically resolve the issue.

Only time and him affording her some distance resolved the issue, and that flat-out sucked.

She'd left her bedroom light burning. He settled her on the wide, netting-draped bed, and eased her running shoes off. As soon as her feet were free, she rolled to the middle of the fluffy white comforter, gave the baggy running shorts she wore a restless tug, and then curled into a fetal position that put her back to him. The shorts draped low on her hips, and her jog tank rode up several inches. For about half a second, he considered stripping her out of the little shorts and top, but decided against it. However sandy her clothes might be, a little discomfort wouldn't kill her, but the sight of Quinn Sheridan sprawled naked over a big, roomy bed might do him in.

Right. Time to go. He had to stop noticing how the glow from the bedside lamp highlighted the shallow V of ass cleavage peeking out from above those low-riding shorts. Stop imagining kissing her just there and then running his tongue up every inch of her spine until he reached the fine hairs at the nape of her neck. Stop standing over her like a fucking creeper. He retreated to the kitchen to grab a bottle of water on his way out, but then snagged one for her as well. It was the least he could do, he justified, as he climbed the stairs, considering she hadn't abandoned him on the beach. Subjecting himself to another eyeful of Quinn all pliant, relaxed, and unaware was far less of a threat to his sanity than conscious, deliberately seductive Quinn.

As soon as he walked back into her bedroom, he realized how wrong he'd been. Pliant, relaxed, unaware Quinn had kicked the covers to the foot of the bed and shucked off her running shorts sometime over the last two minutes, and was now face down on the sheets, snoring lightly into a pillow, with the shorts tangled around one ankle and her bare ass taunting him with its pale perfection.

In his mind, he saw himself crawl over the mattress, brace his arms on either side of that vulnerable prize, and coax her awake slowly, by degrees, with fleeting kisses, and teasing breaths until she arched and moaned in her sleep, begging for more. Then he'd introduce tongue, and teeth, to drive her higher, pull the need tighter. And then, when she put it all right there within his reach, he would *wake* her—whip her straight out of her dreams and into an orgasm so real, she'd scream his name before she even opened her eyes. Then, Jesus, then he'd flip her around and…

"Lizard," she mumbled, flinging an arm across the mattress.

And they were having very different dreams right now. He took a painful step closer, and put the water bottle on the nightstand before leaning over and smoothing her hair from her cheek. "Shh. No lizards."

Then he pulled the sheet over her, turned off the light, and retreated. On his way out of the villa, he faced up to one final truth he hadn't managed to confront earlier in the evening. He was a hard-charging, take control kind of person. When he wanted something, he went after it with discipline and intensity until he achieved the goal. It wasn't in his nature to back off. But when their time here ended, he would have to back the fuck off and give Quinn space. Being fair to her, and to him, meant letting her figure out what she wanted, and needed, once she was free of the cage.

Chapter Twelve

"Your brother wants to come see you."

Quinn took her phone off speaker and lifted it to her ear. A pang of…something…tightened her stomach. "Mom, no. Impossible."

Her mother sighed. "Honey, he's lonely at Foundations, and I think a change of scenery would do him wonders. You've got a big villa all to yourself."

"I'm lonely, too"—spending evenings by herself, reciting lines to an empty room and regretting an apparently unrequited attachment to a certain hard-assed trainer tended to do that to her—"but I'm not on vacation. I've got less than two weeks to finish prepping for my role, and I don't have time to entertain Callum. Besides, I'm not an addiction specialist."

"You don't need to be. They have them on Paradise Bay. You just need to be a supportive sister."

"His doctors recommend shuttling him here for a change of scenery?" Frustration leaked through in her tone. "Because nobody from Foundations reached out to me with the request."

"Of course not. To them, he's simply another client, and they recommend he stick with their program. But you know how much it would mean to him, and you'd be a positive influence..."

"Gee, Mom, remember how well it worked out last time I tried to be a positive influence?" She meant Callum falling off the wagon and ending up back in rehab. Her parents had no idea he'd messed her knee up in the process.

"A week, Quinn. I'm not asking you to let him move in with you again, but surely you can spare him one measly week?"

"I can't, even if I thought it was a good idea." Unfocused energy propelled her up from the sofa, and into the kitchen. "I'm here to work. An entourage isn't permitted." She didn't even want to think about how Luke would react if her brother suddenly arrived on the scene. Tempting as it was to give in to family pressure, and, yes, her own chickenshit desire for a buffer, or a security blanket, or a way to distract herself from the harsh truth that she'd fallen head-over-heels for a man who saw her mainly as a debt to repay, she couldn't do it. She'd have to cope with her bruised heart on her own. Since her awkward apology on the beach, Luke had been making it easy—or diabolically difficult—by keeping their interactions steadfastly professional and otherwise keeping his distance.

"Callum is *not* your entourage. He's your brother, and he loves you."

She jerked the refrigerator open. "I love him, too, which is why I told him I'd treat him to a vacation here, or anywhere else he wanted to go, once he finished his program and I finished the movie." Bottled water and raw broccoli spears were not going to fill the gnawing hole in her gut. She slammed the fridge and sagged against it. "A few months from now, he'll be nearly a year clean and sober, hopefully reclaiming his life, and I'll have time to actually hang out with him. Deferring until then gives us both something to look forward to."

"A reward months away isn't going to cut it. He needs something now. Imagine what the last several weeks have been like for him, stuck in the same place, surrounded by the same faces. You know as well as I do, a stagnant environment depresses creative souls. And depression undermines his recovery."

"His constant urge to escape from whatever's going on in his head undermines his recovery," she argued, and approached the fresh goody basket some uninformed member of the housekeeping staff had left on the kitchen island. "He's made progress, but he's coming up on a milestone, and shit's getting tough. His commitment is wavering." She placed the small bunch of bananas on the counter. "This is so textbook even I can diagnose it." Two apples followed. "He needs to buckle down and learn how to deal with life—including the inevitable boring, lonely, and depressing parts—not look for a quick, painless eject out of a situation he doesn't like."

"Easy for you to say, Quinn. You're steadier than he is. You always were, right from the start. You don't have his flashes of brilliance, but you don't suffer the same lows, either. He came out of the womb needing more support. More attention. And if he can't get it from the people who care about him, he'll satisfy the craving somewhere else, in a less positive way."

The double-edged words barely stung her anymore. In Ann Sheridan's eyes, Callum would forever be the fragile genius, and Quinn the determined worker bee, overcoming her natural mediocrity through sheer strength of effort. And to an extent, their mother saw them fairly. But fair or not, she didn't have enough strength to be her brother's safety net. "So what you're saying is, if Callum quits rehab and relapses, it's my fault?" The empty feeling in her stomach yawned as she waited for a reply. She picked a mango from the basket and squeezed it like a stress ball.

"I'm saying we're his family, and he needs our help."

"I *have* tried to help him." She put the mango on the counter and pawed through the remaining items. A couple snack-sized bags caught her eye. "I gave him a place to live." She plucked out one bag—roasted plantain chips. "When that went south, I gave him access to the best rehab facility my money could buy." She lifted the other bag—toasted coconut chips with sea salt and caramel. Sweet. Salty. Forbidden. Her mouth watered. "I don't have anything else to give. Not right now. If Callum stays put, if he realizes nobody's going to rescue him from himself, I think there's a decent chance he'll ride out this phase and learn how to manage the lows."

"I'll come with him."

"That doesn't change my mind. Look, if you and Dad believe Callum needs a vacation from Foundations I can't stop you from—"

"Your father refuses to discuss it. He just buries himself in work and says he can't possibly get away. You know how he is."

Yes, she did. Her father thought it was a terrible idea, but dodged the issue because he didn't want to alienate anyone. Quinn scrubbed her tired eyes. "Right. So here's what's going on, Mom. Dad's sidestepping because he hates to be the bad guy, and you know you can't handle Callum on your own, so you're trying to rope me in."

"He *wants* to come see you. He's begging me. He says he's not going to make it if he doesn't get out of that place for a little while. You're twins. You have a special bond."

"He wants to escape. At this particular point in time, you can't trust him to know what he needs. You have to trust the experts. He can do this, Mom. He can do this if he commits."

Her mother's sigh flowed over the line. "You honestly believe he can do this on his own?"

"Yes. He's not as fragile as you think."

And I'm not as strong, she silently added.

"I hope you're right," her mother replied before she disconnected.

Amazing. Quinn blinked at her now-dormant phone, sitting on the counter looking harmless. Yet, somehow, in the course of a single transmission from the seemingly innocuous device, she'd managed to become solely responsible in the event Callum opted not to stick with Foundations.

The unfairness of it ate at her. She'd been the one to call him on using again. She'd been the one to perform the intervention. She'd been the one to herd him into rehab, and still had the scars to prove it. She was the one who enrolled him in the best facility available, and she was the one hustling to pay the bills. The only thing she *couldn't* do was complete the damn program for him. But by refusing to help him leave, she'd assumed all the risk of his failure in the eyes of their family.

Somehow, she'd also managed to open the bag of coconut chips and pour herself a handful. Her stomach rumbled in anticipation.

One little bite. Just one.

The *Dirty Games* producers would never know. Eddie would never know. Willpower slipped through her fingers like sand. Luke would never know.

You'll know. Just like you know you'll finish the whole bag, and probably the other one, too. Do you really want to sabotage yourself for a moment of...of...?

Holy shit.

She dumped the chips on the counter and picked up her phone. Her wallpaper—a collage of the God-awful "Before" pictures Luke had taken the first day—disappeared as her fingers flew across the screen, dialing a number she'd never called but knew by heart. A deep voice picked up after the first ring.

"Quinn?"

"I…um…I know why I ate the cookies."

"Tell me."

"For comfort." To her horror, the reply came out on a sob.

"Do you need comfort now?" he asked quickly.

Jesus. She ought to say no and let him off the hook. If not for the sake of her pride, then because any other man with a hysterical woman on the other end of the line would run for the hills. "Y-yes."

"I'll be right there."

• • •

Quinn answered the door wearing a silky white Playground at Paradise Bay bathrobe and a wrecked expression. He stepped inside, pulling her into his arms at the same time he kicked the door shut. She buried her tear-streaked face against his chest and clung to him while sobs shook her petite frame. This wasn't an act, or an attempt to manipulate him in some way. This was real heartache.

I miss you, too…

Ah, shit. His heart started to pound, even as his body reacted in the usual ways to the feel of her pressed against him. He felt every line of her through the thin robe. He lifted her into his arms and carried her into the villa, past the chip-strewn kitchen island, and on through to the living area with its oversize, white furniture and view of the dusky courtyard. At the foot of the sofa, he set her on her feet, and then, because he couldn't help himself, he ran a hand over her hair as he murmured, "Shhh. Stop crying."

Whoever he is, he's not worth it.

"I-I can't." She coughed the words out, and he heard the utter despair in them.

The door holding back every jealous impulse, every dangerous urge, every complicated emotion he harbored toward this woman groaned to contain them. He cupped her head and eased it away from his chest, then smoothed her hair back from her face. "Yes, you can. Come on. You're all right."

Tears continued their steady stream down her damp cheeks. Her wet lips trembled apart on a harsh, semi-hysterical noise somewhere between a laugh and a cry. "I am *not* all right. You knew as much as soon as Eddie contacted you."

"That's not true. Stop crying, Quinn, for both our sakes." He'd overestimated himself. The robe swam on her, and somewhere between her crying jag, and his carrying her inside, the tie at her waist had turned to a loose knot. The front gaped a little more every time she took a shuddery breath, and the slippery fabric slid like a lover over her breasts, outlining her defined nipples. The fact that she wasn't trying to entice him didn't stop his mind from racing. In less than a second, he could have the edge flicked aside to bare those perfect breasts, take one tight peak into his mouth and comfort her until she forgot all about some fuckwit who had the power to make her cry from thousands of miles away.

"It is true." She punctuated the remark with a watery sniff. "You wanted nothing to do with me."

Restraint always came easy, except with her. The hinges on his self-control snapped. He spun her around and bent her over the back of the overstuffed white upholstered chair that still bore the imprint of her body. A script was tossed on the matching ottoman. "You think you know what I want?"

Her quick inhale didn't quite cover the rasp of his zipper

as he tore at the front of his jeans. She angled her head so she could look at him. Her eyes were round in her tearstained face as she watched him dig a condom out of his wallet and tear it open. "Luke?"

"Do you?" He rolled the condom on, and then wrapped a fist around his cock and shoved the back of her robe up to her waist. "You think you know what I wanted to do with you as soon as I heard that precise, go-fuck-yourself voice on the other end of a phone?"

She parted her legs and rose up onto her toes. "Do it now."

"Stop crying, and I'll do anything you ask." *Don't think about anyone else while I'm inside you.*

"Help me stop."

The plea barely passed her lips before he drove into her—so deep, he jostled a low, grateful cry from her as she reared up to meet the thrust. He drew back just enough to get a view of how brutally thick he looked lodged inside her smaller, far more delicate body, and then he thrust again, trying to temper the force this time, but still pushing her hips higher over the top of the chair. Her mouth fell open, then slowly closed on a moan as she lowered her head to the cushion.

"You need comfort?" He growled the question.

"Yes," she gasped, her cheek brushing the upholstery as she nodded.

Every reason why this was wrong faded. He could justify anything, because her tears had stopped. "Take it. Take what you need."

Use me.

He forced himself to still, and watched her slowly circle her hips, pulling away at the zenith and then sliding back. When she brought her ass close, despite his best intentions to let her do what she chose, he gave in to the imperative to move, slamming their bodies together and sending her scrambling to stabilize herself. She hadn't quite managed when he thrust into her again. Her toes left the ground. The robe pooled around her shoulders as her body tipped forward. The angle pinned her head and arms to the seat of the chair, and her opportunity for taking ended. This position foreclosed any ability on her part to be an active participant. She could only receive. Whatever comfort he chose to give, in whatever manner he chose to give it. Recipient.

Quinn being Quinn, the limitation didn't stop her from trying to assert control. "Hard, and fast. I don't want to think. I don't want to feel anything but this."

His body accepted the challenge and he proceeded to give her exactly what she asked for, keeping the pace furious, even when her breath hitched, and her body stiffened. Even when an orgasm squeezed every part of her until she sagged into the chair, panting and wrung out.

More.

That's all he could think. Give her more. Make her take more. They'd crossed the line. There was no coming back from this, and he needed to make sure she understood where they stood now. Make sure she looked him in the eye and whimpered his name in acknowledgment the next time she came, so she had no room to maneuver when he asked her the tough questions she'd been evading for weeks. No backpedaling. No throwing up shields. No walking away.

Concentrating on the look-him-in-the-eye part of the plan, he pulled out of her. The abrupt move splashed hot, damp remnants of her orgasm onto her thighs. Her shocked gasp held a note of betrayal, and he felt the sting of it along every inch of his cock.

Prolonged suffering wasn't part of his plan, for either of them, so he hauled her off the chair, spun her around, and braced her high against the wall. Then, knees bent, he slid into her again. His penetration sent a shiver through her.

Her post-orgasmic flush deepened, staining her cheekbones almost the same shade as her lips. Dark-blond lashes sank low over dazed eyes, and her thick sigh of pleasure misted his face.

"Look at me," he managed to say through the crippling chaos of his own need. And then, he simply closed one hand along the side of her head, the other along her jaw, and tipped her face to his. The mouth he'd been dreaming of hovered less than an inch from his. His lips ached to close the distance. His tongue tingled with anticipation of finally exploring the sweet recess his cock had usurped the honor of entering first. "What did you need tonight, Quinn?"

"Comfort." She squirmed her hips as she said it, clearly seeking more. "Something to take away the ache."

He leaned in, offering her more, bringing their mouths infinitesimally closer. "Does this comfort you?" He rocked his hips.

"Yessss."

Her head tried to fall back, but he kept it forward. Kept their eyes locked. "Good." He rocked again, giving her a quick, shallow stir, and then let her chase his retreating cock, so they'd both appreciate the honesty of her response.

"Yes."

The first orgasm had left her sensitive. One hard grind was all she could stand before she dug her heels into his calves for leverage, and lifted.

This time he pursued, pinning her hips to the wall and burying himself high inside her—hilt to clit. She fought it a little, battling the intensity, but then relaxed as he eased back. Her forehead rested against his. Her soft moan assured him that while he might have inflicted more than he thought she could withstand, it worked for her. "When you need comfort, you come to me. Understand? If you feel empty, don't sabotage yourself to fill the void. Don't reach for quick fixes that are going to fail you in the long run. You reach for me, Quinn, because I'm never going to fail you. Say it."

"You. I reach for you."

He rewarded that breakthrough with a surge of his hips. Her lips were a hairsbreadth from his. He could almost feel them. Almost taste them. "That's right. I'll fill every void. Take away every ache. All you have to do is call for me." He needed to see it. See her lips forming his name.

"Luke. Lu—"

And that was it. More than he could take. After struggling for an eternity to deny himself, the war ended here. He captured those lips while his name still lingered on them. Her mouth moved under his, as demanding, and giving as he'd known it would be. He delved deep. She sealed her lips around his tongue, and speared her fingers into his hair, holding him there as if she honestly feared he could abandon the kiss. She'd learn. He tightened his hold on her jaw and lunged into her again, claiming her everywhere. Claiming everything. Giving everything.

Her hands rushed over him—down his back, under his T-shirt, along his spine—urging him on. A blunt but steady thumping alerted some distant part of his brain that he was buffeting her between the wall and his body, driving into her with more energy than finesse. Fingernails raked his skin.

Too rough. He was being way too rough.

He got a hand under her, supporting her, his fingers sinking into the divide between her ass cheeks. She ripped her mouth from his and whimpered his name as she quivered on the brink of another orgasm.

He buried his face in the curve of her neck, and shot them both over the edge, groaning in surrender as something far too annihilating to be relief shuddered through him.

Chapter Thirteen

"Comfort comes at a price, Quinn. Pay up. Talk to me."

She didn't remember sliding down the wall, but somehow she'd ended up on Luke's lap, her legs slung around his hips, her arms clinging to shoulders, and her head crashed on his chest. Her body suffered a thousand tender spots, but right now, before they exchanged any serious words, her heart wasn't one of them. All the aches were deeply satisfying, like sore muscles after a good workout. Talking would ruin the rarified state. She raised her head and gave him her brassiest smile. "I think we pretty much covered everything worth discussing."

Not even a ghost of a smile greeted her. "Think again."

Retreat seemed like her next best option. She made a move to crawl off his lap, only to find big hands banded around her arms. "Think again," he repeated.

She opened her mouth to tell him to...what, she wasn't sure...but the disaster comprising the last six months of her life started dribbling out in a halting, unrehearsed order—tonight's call with her mother segued into her brother's long friendship with coke, and her failed effort to help him relaunch his life after his last attempt at getting clean. The more she talked, the more impossible it became to stem the flow of words. Like a dam with a hairline crack, each escaping detail weakened the wall behind which she held everything at bay. It crumbled slowly at first, and then quickly, in a rush that sounded disjointed even to her. Poor Luke didn't have a chance in hell of following every stream of her rambling explanation, but he didn't interrupt with questions or attempt to bring order to the information. He just let her talk. And she did, unable to stop even as the bitter truth about her knee sprain spewed out.

"Jesus." She shut her eyes and pressed her hand to her mouth, but it was too late. "Nobody knows that," she added quickly. "Not my parents. Not Eddie. I don't want anyone to know. Please, don't tell anyone."

"Shhh." Something touched her face. His thumb, sweeping away more tears she hadn't realized escaped. "Like everything you tell me, this stays between us. You can trust me. You did the right thing by telling me."

She took over the job of mopping her face, but still didn't look at him. "I don't feel right. I feel like a fucking train wreck. I'm not supposed to come apart like this. Callum's the one prone to shatter. I'm supposed to be the strong one. My mother thinks I should let him come. My brother thinks—"

"I don't give a goddamn what either of them think. It's off the table."

Now she did look at him, taking in his steely eyes and set jaw. His edict, and the arrogance with which he'd delivered it, should have pissed her off, but it didn't. He made her feel… protected. Especially when he added, "If you need someone else to point to for reasons, point to me, because if he comes anywhere near you, I'm kicking his ass."

He took a breath and visibly banked his temper, while

her heart slid a little farther out of her grasp. As a rule, she didn't inspire protective instincts in…well…anybody. There were reasons she played the kind of roles she did. She *was* tough. Her family expected it. Her profession demanded it. Seeing Luke's tightly reined temper rise on her behalf hit squarely in some soft underbelly of her emotional armor she tried her best to keep hidden.

"You don't owe him any favors, Quinn. You did him a big one by not pressing charges, and putting him in a program instead of a jail cell."

Defending her brother came automatically. "He didn't mean to hurt me. He just…couldn't stay on his feet. He couldn't control himself."

"And as long as he's battling an addiction, he's not in control. He's in a world of hurt. His request tells me he's desperate for a way out of his situation, and not above manipulating the people who love him to find one. Desperate people get careless and mean. Don't put yourself in harm's way again. Keep your distance until you're both sure of his motives. Make him earn your trust."

"Is that an order?"

She immediately regretted the bristly retort. His support eased the guilt and uncertainty clawing at her. This once, she wanted someone she could trust to tell her what to do. And she trusted him.

Apparently he realized as much, even if she lacked the good grace to say it out loud. He squeezed her fingers before releasing her hand. "A strict order."

He can read you like a comic book.

A frightening thought, when she really considered it. Could he see everything, like how far gone she was where he was concerned? And just how the hell did *he* feel? Yes, he'd just fucked her blind, but she knew better than to read anything into that. She'd used sex like a weapon from day one, to balance the scales, get under his skin, and, at times, just prove to herself he wasn't immune to her. He'd already proved he wasn't above engaging in some sexual brinksmanship of his own.

And no, she wasn't playing anymore. Over the past weeks, things had changed for her. But for him? Unlikely. If anything, her breakdown tonight probably cemented his opinion of her as a head case. She busied herself straightening and securing her robe—rebuilding her smooth facade—and mustered up some actual manners. "I'm sorry I interrupted your evening with my personal drama. Thank you for dropping everything and coming over to..." Fuck me? "...comfort me."

"You call. I come. That was always part of the deal."

She snuck a look at him from under her lashes. "Am I so predictable? You knew it was only a matter of time before a neurotic narcissist like me needed even more attention?"

He ran his index finger down the front of her robe, edging the fabric aside to bare her breast. "You are definitely not predictable. Quinn, I think you know the rest of what occurred tonight wasn't part of our deal. It wasn't supposed to happen."

Exactly what a girl wanted to hear from the man who'd just made her come so hard, she'd seen stars. Her nipple tightened under his gaze as if to dispute him, even as a dull throb settled in her chest. "Because I'm a client?"

"That's what you're supposed to be, according to the contract we both signed. But that's only part of the reason."

"Sounds like you've got a whole list." She drew back and attempted to cover herself and get her feet under her at the same time. Listening to a rundown of her shortcomings was more than she could handle right now.

He caught a handful of the front of her robe and anchored her in place. "It got a lot shorter, as of a minute ago."

"You know what, Luke? You can take your list and shove

it up your—"

"The day your brother called, I overheard you telling him you missed him. I thought you were hung up on some guy. An ex."

"Wow. I'm a neurotic, narcissistic, lying cheater. That's pretty low, even for me. I told you I wasn't involved with anyone. Do you really think I'd get on my knees for you if I was?"

Some emotion she couldn't name lit the gold around his pupils. "I didn't think you were involved with him. I thought you had feelings for him. Which you do, as it turns out, but I misinterpreted the situation. I've been tearing myself up for weeks because of it."

Her heart stuttered, and then took off at double-time. She rested her hands on his shoulders and leaned in close enough to watch his pupils expand. "What are you saying to me, Luke McLean?"

He whipped her robe open again and they both watched his big, tanned hand cup her pale breast. "I'm saying the thought of you missing an ex drove me crazy." The admission came out in a tight, tortured voice. He kneaded her flesh possessively. "The idea that you might be longing for another man's hands on you while you were here with me made me burn from the inside out."

His words were making *her* burn from the inside out. "You were…jealous?"

He moved his hand to the place where her heart pounded. "As fuck. That crosses all kinds of lines, Trouble, and I know it, but I was jealous as fuck."

Her arms were around his neck before she knew she meant to hug him. As emotions went, his confession of jealousy fell far short of what she felt for him, but her eager heart was willing to accept inspiring his territorial impulses as a start. "I don't care about the lines." She didn't. His lines were ridiculous as far as she was concerned. To demonstrate, she grabbed the hem of his shirt and lifted. He raised his arms and let her drag it off.

"I care. But I'll deal with the lines we have left." Before she could question his cryptic vow, he settled her astride his lap. "Trust me." He nudged her forward and trailed his mouth along her jaw while she shivered at the way their bodies fit so perfectly together.

His low voice vibrated in her ear. "Trust me."

• • •

Luke sat on the end of his favorite lounge chair in the courtyard of Quinn's villa, watching the first rays of dawn gild the clouds lined up across the sky, and holding his phone to his ear. Eddie's cautious voice filled it, providing the wrong soundtrack for memories of Quinn kneeling between the chairs and showing him how much she appreciated imported chocolate ice cream.

"When I asked for a favor," Eddie continued, "I didn't expect you to do it for free. You took a six-week hiatus from your business, dropped everything to go to Paradise Bay and train my client. It wasn't a vacation. You've spent time and incurred expenses. You're entitled to receive the compensation called for under the contract. Are you sure you want to do this, man?"

Gold deepened to fire, tingeing sky and water pink. He'd get Quinn in the water today. Maybe a beach run for cardio, and then a swim to cool down and work some muscle groups besides her legs. After that? Quinn, wet and panting…the possibilities abounded.

"Luke?"

Eddie's voice brought him back to the here and now. He wasn't prepared for this debate, mainly because he hadn't expected his friend to pick up at such an early hour. He'd aimed to leave a message and avoid explanations. "I'm sure. Cancel the contract. I'm waiving my fees and absorbing the expenses. My business manager will refund the deposit. I'm not charging Quinn for this."

Luke heard a mattress groan, like someone shifting to sit up in bed, and then an unfamiliar murmur from the other end of the line. Shit. Had Eddie been…entertaining? Confirmation came quickly as his friend said, "Couple bottles of Ace in the wine fridge. Help yourself. Pour me a glass while you're at it. I'll be down soon."

A moment passed, presumably while Eddie waited for his guest to exit, and then he continued. "What's going on? I thought you told me everything was on track. I grant you, I've only seen her over FaceTime, but she looks great. Are you telling me at five weeks into this, you're not going to hit the goal?"

"Not at all. She's done an amazing job. If you want to measure the success of this effort strictly by BMI, we'll do the fifth week assessment on Friday and I expect she'll be within a percentage point of her target. Relax, Eddie. She's there. If the producers saw her today, the out clause would never enter their minds. Their only concern would be getting her in front of the cameras as soon as possible."

"Okay. That's a relief. But then why are you killing the contract?"

"Because I don't get involved with clients."

"What's that got to do with anything? Ah. Never mind. I retract the question."

"Yeah. *Ah*. It's not a problem if she's not a client."

"That's a huge fucking forfeit on your part…"

"I've done the math—"

"…especially if you're just being a stickler. You two indulged in a one-off? You're both consenting adults. Call it a moment of personal time, and get back to work. Ten days from now, she won't be a client."

"I'm not being a stickler, you cynical bastard. It wasn't a one-off. We're *involved*." Exasperation turned his voice terse. "I didn't plan it, but it happened, and I can't undo it."

"This is probably a good point for me to mention that Quinn's not just one of my favorite clients, she's one of my favorite people. I sent her to you, so I'm also going to say this. She deserves some fucking enthusiasm, not a guy with no plan who's trying to 'undo' a personal mistake with a professional sacrifice."

Fair enough. He let out a breath and rubbed the back of his head. He didn't mean to come off like an unwilling victim. All the hesitancy he felt was on her behalf. She deserved a chance to consider her feelings in a couple weeks when real life resumed, and decide if this was really what she wanted. But he hadn't given it to her. His plans moving forward didn't involve giving it to her, and deep down, he had no regrets. "Even if I could undo it, I wouldn't want to. Quinn's not a mistake."

"All right. Fine." Eddie paused for a moment—the mating calls of a few die-hard Coqui frogs filled the silence—and then he added, "I've worked with her since she was a kid. I know she's not a kid anymore, but she's also not as tough and jaded as she comes off."

Luke leaned against the painted wood railing and turned his face into the salty breeze. "I know exactly what she is." A headstrong, smart-mouthed, compassionate, talented, hardworking pain in his ass, and he'd fallen in love with her.

"She's also about to hit the next level in a business you want nothing to do with. Just winning the Lena Xavier role put all kinds of heat on her. I'm seeing a *Dirty Games* updraft like you wouldn't believe, and when filming and promotion start, it will get even crazier. Projects roll in every day. Good projects. She sings, she dances, and she acts. Talent and versatility, wrapped up in the kind of package the camera loves. Her trajectory is straight up. There's no undoing *that*, either."

"And I wouldn't ask her to. Look, I appreciate your concern"—not really, but he recognized Eddie was trying to look out for her—"but we both know I understand what I'm signing up for. Do I love the Hollywood game? No. It's a big hustle, as far as I'm concerned. But she wants to play, so we'll work it out."

"For the record, you're one of my favorite people, too."

"Aw. Now you're making me blush."

"You're also a sarcastic prick," he replied, "but I have confidence Quinn can serve the sarcasm right back to you in spades. You two could be good for each other, but don't let the fact that she came to you as a client delude you into thinking you're in charge. In my experience, relationships and unilateral decisions don't mix. Especially not ones that set you back, financially. Paradise Bay has a lot to recommend it, but cost isn't one of them. Your expenses alone could choke a horse. Can you afford to take this kind of hit, just to avoid some optics that make you uncomfortable?"

The loss dwindled his cash reserve to a stingy level, but he'd manage. "The optics matter."

"Have you discussed this with her? Or considered what the optics look like to her? I guarantee she's going to see things differently."

"I'll square it with her. Tear up the contract, Eddie. There are a lot of things I'll accept from Quinn, but money isn't one of them."

Chapter Fourteen

Quinn woke slowly, languishing in the hazy space between dream and reality. The dreams were hard to leave—a low voice rolling over like a velvet caress, a big hand fisted in her hair, strong thighs backstopping hers, and the slap of skin on skin so loud, it still echoed in her ears, along with a strangely familiar hum. Just dreams?

Reality beckoned, each trace registering like a separate clue. Carelessly drawn drapes filtered soft light into her mahogany and whitewashed bedroom. Her outflung arm rested over a warm, yet vacant side of the bed. A side she had a fuzzy memory of lying half out of at one point last night, palms braced on the floor and her hair swinging into her face, obscuring her view of the locally loomed rug while strong hands lifted her hips to various angles to ensure her G-spot got a staggering workout. Speaking of workouts, the barest stretch of her sleep-slackened body set off intimate aches in certain well-used muscles.

The low, familiar hum sounded again and roused her out of her floaty state of grace. This time she placed the sound.

Her phone vibrated on the nightstand. Somebody kept trying to call her, and the noise had finally drawn her out of sleep. She leaned over and grabbed the phone. Her mom's number flashed on the screen, along with the time. Six forty-five in the morning here translated to quarter to four, Pacific time. Alarm bells jangled in her brain, blasting away the last vestiges of lassitude.

"Mom. What's happened?"

"Have you heard from your brother?"

Her stomach clenched. "No." Belatedly, she checked her texts. It didn't change her answer. "Why? What does he need?"

"To be located."

"Located? I don't understand. He's at Foundations—"

"Not anymore. They called last night. He checked out. I thought you chose a reputable facility, Quinn. How could they let him leave?"

Her heart sank under the weight of worry and her mother's censure. "It's not court-mandated rehab, Mom." Yet another mistake on her part? Should she have pressed charges against her own brother, and then begged the judge to order him into a program? "It's a private, voluntary facility and he's an adult. They can't hold him against his will." Her mind scrambled for traction. "Who'd he check out with? Did someone pick them up? Does he have any money?"

"They can't tell me if he left with anyone, due to patient confidentiality rules. I don't know if anyone picked him up. Money? No. And he doesn't have access to any. He ran through his cash years ago. Your father and I have been in no position to replenish his accounts."

Sad, but there it was. She pressed fingers to her temple and ordered herself to *think*. "Okay. All right. Don't panic. I'll call Eddie in a couple of hours and see what he can do." The man hadn't climbed to the upper echelon of sports and entertainment agents without being extremely resourceful, and well-connected. Plus, if Callum was wheeling around Los Angeles without cash, he might put a call in to his former agent. She hoped she could convince Eddie to take the call, just this once.

"That's a good idea. Eddie knows people…and he knows Callum." Her mother already sounded calmer. "He might be able to work some magic."

"I hope." She slumped against the pillows and worried her lip for a second, uncertain whether to offer the words tangled in her throat. Guilt pushed them up. "I can't seem to work any magic where he's concerned. I really thought he'd stick this time if we all stood firm. I should have listened to you. I'm sorry."

Silence greeted her apology. One heartbeat. Two. She braced herself for the recriminations which would drop like thunderbolts from the higher moral ground upon which her mother stood.

Instead she got a long, weary sigh. "No, Quinn. *I'm* sorry. Last night when I spoke to the counselor managing your brother's program, he pointed out that Callum's request for me to arrange his transfer to Paradise Bay amounted to an attempt to spread responsibility for his failure to complete his program to me. He manipulates me very well because I'm susceptible. I take it personally when he fails, and I feel like a terrible parent. Useless, ineffective. I'm his *mother*, for God's sake. *I'm* supposed to have the magic where my child is concerned, but I don't. I just don't. I never did." Her mom's voice broke. "But you did, Quinn. I don't know if it's because you're twins, or what, but sometimes I sensed this special connection between you two, so I tried to…"

Ann's voice broke on a sob, and Quinn rushed to smooth things over. "It's okay."

"It's not okay," her mother replied, sounding steadier.

"What I realized is that I do to you exactly what Callum does to me. I pull you in because I'm desperate to find someone stronger than me to bear the load. It's horribly unfair to you. You're not your brother's keeper."

"Neither are you. He's twenty-three, Mom. All grown up. He makes his own choices, and he has to deal with the consequences. All we can do is offer support when he's ready for real help, but we're not experts. Sometimes it's hard to tell where to draw the line between supporting him and enabling him. We might get it wrong on occasion, but you know what? That doesn't change the underlying fact that Callum is responsible for Callum. I know you're worried about him. I am, too. But even when we find him, there's no dragging him back to Foundations if he doesn't want to go—or anywhere else, for that matter."

"I know." Her mother breathed heavily. "In my heart, I know you're right. It's just so hard, as a parent, to watch your child struggle."

Favorite child, Quinn silently inserted, despite having made her peace with that hierarchy a long time ago. "It's hard for me, too, Mom." She wasn't sure if empathy or self-defense motivated the comment, but her mother wasn't trying to pick a fight, so she added, "You're not alone. We want the same thing for him. We may not see eye-to-eye all the time about how to get there, but, ultimately we're on the same side. His."

"I know that, too. I do, Quinn." A hollow laugh followed. "Some mother I am. I never seem to have the right magic for one of my kids, and the other never needed any. At least not from me. I—Quinn—I'm sorry if I've been holding that against you. You were always so self-directed. So determined. You never undermined yourself the way he does."

Never undermined herself? *Ha*. Someday it might do them both good if she told her mother that wasn't strictly true, but now wasn't the time to dive into her needs and the bad habits they fostered. "You don't have to justify anything. I mean, there's nothing to justify. Magic takes many forms. If I learned to be self-directed, I probably have my parents to thank for it. Same goes for determination. Claim a little more credit for our successes, and a little less responsibility for every stumble, okay?"

"I'll try."

"Good." She ended the call with a promise to get in touch as soon as she talked to Eddie, and an exchange of "I love you's."

Her thumb hovered over the screen as she considered calling him now, and leaving a message, but decided against it. She wanted to speak to him. Better to call the office in a couple of hours. Lisa would make sure she got through, even if he was busy.

She lowered her phone and looked around the empty room. Where was Luke?

Auras and energy currents and psychic links weren't her thing, but she didn't need any woo-woo powers to sense the villa was empty. Luke McLean had left the building. Whatever morning-after fantasy she'd woven last night as she'd fallen asleep in his arms evaporated.

Get over it. This isn't the first time you've woken alone.

It wasn't. But it was the first time she'd cared. Last night he'd told her those hard-and-fast rules he'd been enforcing between them no longer mattered. Heck, together they'd eliminated another hard-and-fast rule—one she liked to refer to as the condom rule—by confirming she was on the pill and they were both risk-free. And for her, at least, that was not a one-night-stand kind of discussion. Had the first cringes of dawn found him regretting his words? Was he sending her a message with his absence?

Cold tendrils of doubt wound their way through her. She straightened her spine and batted them back. Screw that. She intended to deliver a message of her own. Directly. She loved him, dammit. Her insides quivered a little at the thought. She loved the arrogant, bossy, inflexible bastard, and she didn't give a single shit about his lines. She would say her piece, and he would listen, and then, if he didn't feel the same, fine. She'd gather up the slivers of the heart she'd shattered for him, and try her best to put them back together. But if he was backing off out of some misguided notion of not taking advantage of her, she was going to kick his finely chiseled ass.

Blood fired, she tossed the covers back, threw on a robe, and stalked downstairs. When she reached the landing, she heard the murmur of a voice. Through the open doors she saw Luke sitting on the patio, talking on his phone. The realization that he hadn't escaped to his own space settled the boil of her temper to a simmer. She approached, lingering in the doorway to take in the sight of him profiled against the dawn. Bed-rumpled hair, the morning stubble shadowing his jaw, and the soft light caressing the telltale red marks on his shoulders left by her fingernails. A few frayed threads from his wash-worn jeans looked stark against the tanned skin of his foot. Belatedly, she noticed his shirt and shoes on the living room floor, along with her robe from last night. His getaway wardrobe was right there, if he'd been inclined to use it. She looked back at him, talking away in nothing but his haphazardly pulled on jeans. Apparently he wasn't.

She stepped out onto the cobblestone, but he didn't sense her presence. The phone conversation absorbed all of his attention. And hers. She didn't come out with the intention of eavesdropping, but she heard him say her name. Moving closer, she waited while the person on the other end of the line spoke in what reached her ears as a tinny, indecipherable ramble.

Luke's response, however, was clear enough. "I'll square it with her. Tear up the contract, Eddie. There are a lot of things I'll accept from Quinn, but money isn't one of them."

Tear up the contract? *Their* contract? Something he'd said last night replayed in her mind.

I'll deal with the lines we have left.

She waited patiently and silently while he concluded the call, and then asked, "What did you just do, Luke?"

The hesitation of his thumb over the screen of his phone offered the only outward indication she'd startled him. He raised his head and turned to look at her, eyes calm, but full of resolve.

He didn't need to respond. The pieces of the puzzle were falling into place. Her real question wasn't what, but *why*. "Why did you tell Eddie to cancel our contract?"

• • •

Paradise Bay ought to hire Quinn to model their robes. They'd sell a million with a single image of her standing in the courtyard with her hair tumbling down in sexy disarray, and her body drenched in white silk that the first rays of daylight turned semitransparent. Fierce eyes glared with what could, at first glance, look like pure, unadulterated sexual heat, but he knew better. She was riled up, all right. To fight.

"You know why." He stood, and slid his phone into the back pocket of his jeans. "Feel free to argue yourself breathless. It won't change anything."

She crossed her arms and lifted her chin, but he caught a shadow of something else in the blue depths of her eyes. Anxiety? Fear? Instinct told him to drill down on it. He closed the distance between them, and took her proud little chin in a light grip. "What's wrong?"

"You just took a big loss, because of me. What's right about that?"

Okay. Apparently they'd have to get through this first.

"This is what's right about it." He covered her stubborn lips with his. A little pressure broke the stern line. They opened on a sigh, and admitted him with the eager escort of her tongue. He moved in, bodily, holding the back of her neck, cupping her ass through the slippery silk, trapping her against him until slender thighs parted for his and lush breasts plumped against his chest. Quick hands trespassed into the back of his jeans, and held. Her heartbeat vibrated through him like an echo of his own. When he lifted his head, she didn't move, except to let out a soft breath.

"I can't think when you do that to me."

And he could, with her snuggled against him, head tipped back, lips wet and swollen from his kisses? "You don't need to think right now." He kissed her again, and again, suddenly starved for the hot slide of her mouth under his. Following a half-formed notion of laying her out on the chair where she'd bestowed one of his fondest memories and returning the favor, he turned them and then backed her up a step.

His phone pinged from his pocket, signaling a text.

She froze. He cursed. "That's Eddie. Don't worry about it."

Wide, serious eyes stared up at him. She stepped out of his arms and wrapped hers around herself. "I do worry. Luke, I know you think you crossed some kind of line with me, and… look, I don't know if you're canceling the contract to make this better for you, or for me, but either way, it's crazy. It's not fair to you, and I'm not okay with it. You provided me with your time and professional expertise. I got the benefit of both. You *earned* your fees. We have a professional relationship—"

"No." He shook his head. "We never had a professional relationship. We were far over that boundary before we even got started."

"You didn't want me as a client."

"I sure as hell didn't," he agreed. "Any more than you

wanted me as a trainer. But I wanted *you*."

"A neurotic, narcissistic actress," she said softly.

"Seems I've got a weakness for your kind of trouble, Trouble."

He understood what she was pointing out, though. Not every issue was solved by tearing up a few sheets of paper. She loved what she did. She excelled at it, and he was going to have to deal with her career if he wanted this to work. If he couldn't, then canceling the contract really was just a pride-saving sacrifice on his part. "You're mine."

He wanted to say more, tell her more, but more wasn't fair to her. Not yet. Despite being thousands of miles from home, they weren't on neutral ground. They were on his turf. And despite canceling the contract, they weren't on equal ground. Telling her he wanted her was one thing. She'd made no secret of wanting him, too. But as long as she was relying on him to attain her goal, telling her he was falling in love with her smacked of emotional blackmail. He'd convinced her she needed him, and used it as a mechanism for gaining her compliance. But forcing his feelings on her now took unfair advantage of that need. He could eliminate the contract, but he couldn't eliminate the rest of it quite as easily. He'd have to be patient. "You're mine, and it has nothing to do with a contract. I don't want it between us."

Pink crept into cheeks. "Luke, I love a grand gesture as much as the next girl, but this has real consequences for you. For your business. Are you sure you know what you're doing?"

"It will work out. I have a contingency plan." He'd have to hustle a bit, cut back on his personal time to take on some additional clients, but he'd manage. "I'm not worried." He ran a thumb over the line between her brows. "You shouldn't, either." But neither his words nor his touch made the line disappear. He eased back and took in the stiff set of her shoulders. Time to tackle whatever had put the anxious shadows in her eyes. "Something else on your mind?"

She nibbled her lower lip, clearly debating.

Frustration roughened his voice. "Tell me, Quinn. You don't need a contract in place to trust me with whatever's worrying you."

"I got a call from my mom this morning." Then, on a long exhale, she spilled out the rest, ending with, "I probably ought to call Eddie now, since he's awake, and let him know what's going on."

Luke pulled his phone from his pocket, hit the number for her, and handed it over. He waited again while she paced the courtyard and ran through the situation for Eddie, listened to her respond to a few questions, and add a grateful, "Thanks. I really appreciate this."

Eddie spoke again, and apparently shifted the conversation, because Quinn stopped wearing a path along the cobblestones and turned her attention to him. "Yeah. He told me." Eddie said something more, and she laughed. Her first real laugh of the morning. "Yes, I realize I still have to do what he tells me to do." She sent a smirk his way. "For another week. Then he can do what *I* say for a change."

He simply lifted his brows in reply, but battled back the smile that kept trying to lift the corners of his mouth at her casual reference to a future with him once she returned to real life. Only an idiot would read too much into the comment—especially one intended more as a joke than a guarantee—but he read it as a good sign anyway. When she said good-bye and handed the phone back to him, he took stock of her. She looked better. Not cool, scratch-resistant Quinn Sheridan by a long shot, but less upset.

He aimed to keep the trend going. "What do you say to a beach day?"

Chapter Fifteen

"*This* is your idea of a beach day?"

Quinn extended her arms and straightened her legs until she stood on the bike pedals. The position gained her enough leverage to continue her slow ascent up the millionth steep hill. She could see the beach—seen plenty of it, in fact, during their meandering, three-and-a-half-mile run around the resort to get to the bike rental place, and plenty more during their bicycle trek to the other side of the island. Stupid her, assuming a beach day meant parking her ass on a towel and sticking her toes in sun-warmed sand.

Luke looked back at her, his eyes unreadable behind dark sunglasses, but something in the set of his brows told her he was laughing at her. "This is part of it."

"The *worst* part," she muttered under her breath, and struggled to maintain enough speed to stay upright.

"Keep pedaling. We're almost there."

"There? It's an island," she argued. "We're surrounded by seashore. The resort has its very own beach right on the property. Chilled drinks, full-service cabanas, and best of all, no bike ride required."

"I don't think you really want a bunch of resort guests and staff underfoot when I peel you out of your bikini and apply sunscreen to all your hard-to-reach places."

Oh. Well, maybe not.

"Besides, the view is worth the trip." He faced forward again, and she had to admit the current view did not suck. Late morning sun played over a mouthwatering arrangement of bulging delts, angled traps, and strong scapulae before tapering down long, lean lats partially obscured by the dark-blue backpack strapped to his shoulders. The bulk of it shaded the lower half of his back, casting shadows into twin dimples at the base of his spine. Then he raised his body higher on his bike as well, treating her to an eyeful of rock-hard glutes bunching and flexing under a thin veil of blue and white hibiscus print swim trunks. Sweat darkened the waistband just below the small of his back. She had a quick, naughty urge to tug the damp fabric down and lick the salty skin. Licking and licking so the taste coated her mouth, and then spearing her tongue into the tight crevice at the top of his ass until he cursed and threatened her with toe-curling… consequences.

She was so lost in the fantasy, she almost didn't notice they were cresting the hill. Her speed picked up as she followed Luke down a slight decline, and then squeezed the brake when he said, "This way." He leaned his body into a turn in the absently graceful way of someone accustomed to riding, and disappeared into what looked like a wall of jungle. Seconds later, she coasted to the same spot and saw he'd steered his bike down a dirt path. She followed, clutching the brakes with white-knuckled intensity as greenery whipped by on either side of the narrow, rutted path. Trees and vines formed a canopy above them. The ocean breeze gave way to thicker air, and thicker scents—rain-soaked soil overlaid with a steaming perfume of wild growing fruits, exotic flowers, and an invisible zoo of animals and insects.

Just as her ponderings about the animals and insects part of the equation started to freak her out, the vegetation ended. They shot into sunlight so bright and startling, she blinked behind her polarized sunglasses. Drifts of sand encroached on the path, shushing her tires. She sort of stalled to a stop beside where Luke stood straddling his bike. He took hold of her handlebar in a caretaker move that wasn't necessary, but made her heart stutter anyway.

"What do you think?"

She forced herself to relinquish the sight of his big, masculine hand wrapped around her bike handle, tendons raised in an unconscious show of strength, and looked at her surroundings. The curtain of green they'd traveled through surrounded a small cove. The beach slanted gently down to where knee-high waves foamed out to an iridescent sheen on pearly white sand. Beyond, blue-green water stretched all the way to the horizon. Puffy white clouds sailed there like a distant regatta.

"Breathtaking."

"Yeah."

She turned to find him looking at her, his dark glasses pushed to the top of his head so she couldn't mistake the fact that she was the object of his attention. He was calling her beautiful, and it was nothing she hadn't heard hundreds of times from hundreds of people, but from him, it went beyond an acknowledgment of lucky genetics, or even a compliment. It *meant* something. Or she wanted it to, at least. Swagger was her only defense against that stare of his—the one that saw so much more than she'd ever shown anyone. She dismounted and walked her bike toward an outcrop of rocks. "If you're trying to make me forget you dragged me through the better part of an Ironman under the pretenses of a beach day, you're going to have to try harder."

He walked his bike over and parked it beside hers. The corner of his mouth lifted. "What'd you have in mind?"

"Dance with me." The request flew out of her mouth before she realized what she'd intended to say.

He looked as startled by the request as she was. The breeze rustled through the palms while he shrugged off the backpack. The waves lapped the sand. From the depths of the trees came the warble of birds. "We don't have any music," he finally said, as he unzipped the center compartment and busied himself digging around inside.

"Are you blushing?" Delighted at the thought, she moved closer.

"No." Without looking up, he handed her a towel.

She tossed it to the sand. Her sunglasses and slouchy tank top followed. "I've got at least twenty different playlists on my phone." She didn't give a damn about music. It suddenly occurred to her that she hadn't really danced in months—not since the knee sprain—and she missed it. She felt like dancing, and she wanted his arms around her when she did it. "What's the matter, Luke? Afraid to dance with me? Worried you can't keep up?"

She kicked off her shorts and twirled away, loving the sheer freedom of the movement, knowing her hard-won shape made the most of the little black bikini she'd chosen. Thanks to Luke's coaching…browbeating…whatever, and her own determination, her body had returned to the slender, camera-ready condition she'd taken for granted most of her life. Experimenting, she did a fluid turn and took it into a leap. The familiar weightlessness left her giddy. She landed ankle deep in a wave and sucked in a quick breath as tiny droplets of cool water splashed her.

Deciding to deal with the painful part sooner than later, she leaned over, scooped up handfuls of water, and poured them on her arms, chest, and middle. In the process, she couldn't help noting with satisfaction that five weeks of work and sacrifice were definitely paying off in the form of lean limbs, a flat stomach, and an ass tight enough to star in its own close-up. Weight training had put new definition in her arms and torso. She'd always had dancer's legs, and at this moment, she wanted to use them.

Her chosen partner, however, stood barefoot at the waterline, arms folded across his superhero chest. "Seems like a partner would only get in your way. How about I be the audience?"

He needed convincing? She could be convincing. Especially since she'd caught the admiration in his eyes, not just for her body, but her ability. She wanted more of that. Because they had the spot all to themselves, she did another twirl, whipped off her bikini top in the process, and covered herself with her arm. Aware of his eyes now locked on her partially hidden breasts, she flung the top at his feet. "I prefer audience participation." She skimmed a foot through the surf and kicked water at him.

"Careful what you ask for."

"I don't think I need to be careful." To prove it, she turned her back on him, stretched up onto her toes, and twined her arms behind her head, lifting her hair and letting it tumble down her back. "You know what I *do* think?"

"If you're smart, you'll think about how fast you can run."

"Ha. I think big, bad Luke McLean doesn't know how to dance."

The next instant quick hands spun her around. She found herself caught in strong arms and pulled against unyielding contours of an unmistakably male frame.

A hot, hard ridge carved space for itself along her fluttering stomach. Very male.

Her limbs turned leaden and heat dripped like melted

caramel from low in her abdomen to a place between her thighs.

"This is how I dance," he murmured.

A burly hand sank into the back of her bikini bottoms, cupped her ass, and lifted her. Stranded her against him. "Dirty dancing?" she panted.

His mouth nuzzled her ear. "I guess that's one name for it."

"Okay. I can work with your skillset."

He hitched her higher and let her slide down the length of his cock. "Good to know." His teeth sank into her earlobe.

Her eyelids threatened to close, but she mustered up some willpower and squirmed out of his hold. "Uh-uh. I meant dancing. This is my area of expertise, so I'm in charge. I get to be the trainer. You're the trainee."

The look he gave her told her he was about three seconds from throwing her over his shoulder, carrying her up the beach, and showing her who was in charge. She slapped a hand to the center of his chest and aimed her best *nobody-puts-Baby-in-a-corner* look at him. "Or are you afraid to put all these big, strong muscles at my mercy?"

He lowered his brows in a scowl. "Quinn, I've got two left feet and a dick as hard and heavy as a ten-pound free weight throbbing in my shorts. You really think you've got what it takes to turn me into Patrick Swayze?"

"You bet your two left feet I do. Now take your ten-pound dick and go stand over there."

• • •

Luke waded knee deep into the surf and stood where Quinn indicated. "Here?"

"Face me."

"Never turn your back to the ocean," he grumbled, but

did as she asked. Nothing the Caribbean threw at him could be more dangerous than Quinn standing ten feet away on the sand, wearing a reckless smile and a tiny black scrap of a bikini bottom. Sunlight bathed her, turning her skin luminous, and shimmering off her blond hair like a halo. His chest tightened just looking at her. Words he'd promised himself he wouldn't say yet echoed in his mind. He shook his head to silence them.

"When I say 'up,' I want you to plant your feet, bend your knees a little, and put your arms up like this," Quinn instructed, and raised her hands over her head, palms up, about shoulder width apart. The move lifted her breasts like an offering. His cock jerked so hard, he nearly groaned.

"Like this?"

She nodded. "Perfect." She lowered her arms and backed up several steps, moving diagonally as she went.

Instinctively he turned to keep them head-on. "No, don't move," she said, and waved her hand at him to indicate he should resume his original position. He did. When she was about ten feet away and to his right, she stopped. "Ready?"

"I have no idea."

Her laugh held absolutely no concern. "Just do the thing when I say the word. You'll be fine." With that, she lifted her arms above her head in a graceful arc. Then she was in motion, her moves practiced but easy, like LeBron making a layup. First a small step, followed by a big step, and then she leaped into the air—front leg straight, back leg bent so her toes grazed the ends of her hair.

She stole his breath.

Every line of her body flowed with agile power. The one-legged landing involved some kind of pivot, and next thing he knew she was running straight at him, hair flying, chest bouncing, lips forming a word over and over again, and through a hazy buzz of lust it almost sounded like…

Uuuuuup!

Fuck. He bent his knees and raised his arms as she closed the distance between them. The wave retreated, giving her more runway, and then—holy *shit*—she flew. Literally flew over his head. He caught her by the hips, extended his arms to lock his elbows and stop her forward trajectory. Momentum forced him to take a step back, and then he had her, really had her. Five feet four inches of surprisingly strong, lithe woman balanced like a statue above him.

Triumphant laughter rang in his ears—hers and his—and to keep hers going, he reinforced his grip and spun her in a slow circle. "Oh my God," she shouted, and wrapped her hands around his forearms. "You're a natural."

They hadn't worked on a dismount, but when she let her back relax and lowered her legs, he levered his arms down, tipped his head, and kissed the black triangle covering her sex.

The move wrung a long, indulgent sigh from her.

"You haven't seen the full extent of my talent." Keeping one hand on her hip, he splayed the other along the back of her thigh, and shifted her around until he hitched her leg over his shoulder.

She shrieked and clung to his neck, enveloping his head in a full body hug.

He staggered, then caught himself, and mumbled, "Other leg," against her thigh. "I've got you."

It took her a second to find her balance, but then she leaned back into the hands he had braced under her ass and slung her other leg over his shoulder. He lifted her hips until he could bury his face at the apex of her thighs.

She draped over him, her chin digging into his skull, her arms clasped behind his neck. His lips met damp swimsuit. "Your bikini is soaked. Do I have the ocean to thank for that, or you?"

"Luke..."

He flattened his tongue against the fabric stretched snug over her sex and took a long taste. "You. All you." He tongued her through the suit, his fingers digging into her fleshiest parts when she started to squirm.

Her voice murmured his name in a steady soundtrack of need. A hand fisted in his hair. Legs hooked around his body until the tops of her feet pressed against his ribs. She bucked against his face.

He shoved her closer. Held her there and flayed her relentlessly, until her body stiffened, until he felt that little quiver against his tongue...until her taste flooded his mouth and her scream filled his ears.

A few staggering steps were all he could manage. The lining of his swim trunks threatened to saw his balls off. With a groan of warning, he dropped to his knees in the receding surf, and lowered her to the wet sand.

She rolled over and started crawling the rest of the way out of the water. He caught a handful of her bikini and dragged it down. Her startled breath only heightened the fever. When she looked over her shoulder, the picture she made would have brought him to his knees if he hadn't already been there. Her hair hung in damp tendrils around her orgasm-flushed face and cascaded down her elegant back. The tip of one nipple peeked out from beside her arm. Her soggy swimsuit dangled between her knees, leaving her ass bare save for a dusting of sand low on one cheek where the bottoms hadn't offered any protection.

"Fuck me," someone growled. Him. That tortured animal would be him.

She blinked, and then, as if she had no concern whatsoever for how close he was to losing his mind, she lowered onto her forearms and angled her hips higher. "No, Luke." Her lips curved into an unrepentant smile. "Fuck me."

The pose twisted a fuse inside him, but the smile lit it, and now this slow burn ended only one way—consuming him from the inside out. He wanted to see her sly smile go slack and her blue eyes blur when he pulled her into the fire. He wanted to cover her lips with his, feel every quiver, and taste every sigh as she surrendered to the heat of them. Only chivalry stopped him from flipping her over and driving into her, which would be tantamount to power sanding her backside. Instead he hooked an arm around her waist and rolled, so she ended up sprawled over him.

"Fuck *me*," he said again, and used his foot to tug her bottoms off. He reached around, shoved his trunks down, and gripped his cock. As he nudged it along her cleft, she bit her lip and squirmed.

"Any way you want it, Trouble. Feeling lazy? No problem. Just rest your head on my chest and spread your legs. I'll do all the work to get us both off. Prefer a more active role? Climb on up there and ride me straight into oblivion. Looking for the middle ground? Turn around, hug my knees, and show me how you work that ass. Your choice, but choose fast."

She braced a hand on his chest and pushed herself up so she leaned over him. The position sent her hair falling forward like a silky curtain, and nestled the head of his cock in her folds. With a sweep of her arm, she moved her hair away from her face and locked her eyes on his. "What if I choose all three?"

"You're not going to last through all three." He definitely wasn't. He felt huge to the point of abusive against her softness. Still holding himself at the base, he lifted his hips. She came up higher on her knees, and then sank down slowly, her head tipping back as she took him in to the halfway point.

It was *his* vision that went blurry. He blinked it clear and forced himself to wait like a gentleman, hands supporting her thighs while she rocked back and forth, working him in deeper by increments. When she'd seated herself fully, he let out a breath and prepared himself for a long, easy ride.

He should have known better. Nothing about Quinn was ever easy. She bore down hard and fast, sending a twisted bolt of pain-laced pleasure straight to his balls. His shaft throbbed inside her, brutally thick. The curse on his lips turned into a low groan as she slowly leaned forward, relinquishing half his cock by the time she braced herself on her hands on either side of his head. Her breasts swung forward.

Instinct had him clasping her waist, urging her lower. "Give it to me," he grunted.

"I'm fucking you, remember?" She wiggled her hips. "Any way I want—"

He crunched his abs and raised himself up to capture her breast in his mouth.

"Ohhhh…" Her moan went guttural as he opened wide, drawing her in as deep as possible, scouring the underside of one generous curve with his teeth.

When her moans became whimpers, he allowed her to ease back, letting his teeth rake her tight nipple as she slid free. She automatically brought her hand up to cup the tender flesh. He covered hers with his and squeezed.

Her lips parted. Her breath escaped in pants. Her interior muscles hugged his shaft in quick flutters.

"More," he said, unable to get enough of her, and suddenly, painfully aware the urgency wasn't just physical. He wanted her spark. Her fire. All of her. Promises and commitments—which took them to places he'd sworn he wouldn't go under their current dynamic, because tearing up a contract didn't automatically change his underlying obligations to her. There was a limit to what he could demand from her right now. But he'd go right up to that limit.

"I'm yours," she whispered. "All yours. Take me."

He guided her forward again, bending her lower so her

hips lifted and those flutters concentrated on the head of his cock. She fought herself a little, trying to push her hips back and take him deeper at the same time she stretched to offer him her other breast. He devoured this time, with his whole mouth—his teeth, his tongue—and kept it up until her hips jerked in restless desperation and the flutters turned to hungry clenches.

She speared a hand in his hair, holding his head to her breast, as the clenches turned to spasms and her hips rocked in frantic abandon. "Forever, Luke. Take me forever."

"Don't." But he levered up and captured her mouth, plunged his tongue inside to claim the offer it wasn't fair to accept as her body took him over. He came in a firestorm of need—to take, possess...to keep. All of it burned through him, searing away his resolve and laying him bare. He broke away, pressed his forehead to her jaw, and begged, "Don't say forever unless you mean it, Trouble. I want to hear it too goddamn much."

Chapter Sixteen

I want to hear it too goddamn much.

The words floated to the forefront of Quinn's pleasure-saturated brain, as strong but surprisingly gentle fingers pushed her hair back from her face.

Forever. He wanted forever. With her. She lifted her cheek from his chest and pressed her lips to the spot where his heart thundered. Vaguely, she realized the tide had caught them. Waves swirled over their tangled legs while they lay in the sand like shipwreck survivors washed up on shore.

"You think you can handle forever with a neurotic, narcissistic actress?"

Another hand, not quite as gentle, smacked her ass. Over her startled yelp, he said, "I know exactly how to handle you, Trouble. Think *you* can handle forever with an arrogant fitness Nazi with…what was it again?"

"The world's smallest dick?" She laughed at the memory. "I…um…" Laughter dissolved into a shivering sigh as he slowly slid the dick in question out of her swollen, orgasm-sensitized body. "I might have been wrong about that part."

The comment earned her ass another playful slap. "*Might* have?"

"Ow! Okay. Okay. I was wrong." In self-defense, she reached between them and wrapped her fingers around him. He twitched in her hand. "And yes, I know exactly how to handle you." And then, because this was an important moment, despite how irreverently she'd asked her question, she went on. "I don't need someone to focus solely on me to feel like I matter to them. We both have professional commitments. I don't want to get in the way of yours ever again, or drag you into the middle of mine."

The corner of his mouth lifted into a half smile. "I'm not worried." He ran his thumb along her cheek. "We'll work out the logistics—"

The chime of a phone in the distance put some turbulence under her soaring heart.

"That's you," he said, and gave her butt a reassuring squeeze before releasing it, shifting them both into a sitting position, and handing her waterlogged bikini bottoms back to her.

Indecision tore at her, but family worry won out. She took the bikini and scrambled up. "I better check. Callum might have surfaced."

She snagged her top from the sand on her way to where they'd parked the bikes. Her phone fell silent in the outer pocket of Luke's backpack. After slipping her bottoms on, and looping the top around her neck, she lifted her phone, tapped the screen and saw Eddie had called. A text from him arrived in the next second. Two words, all caps. *CALL ME!*

Sensing Luke behind her, she glanced over her shoulder and tried for calm. "Eddie. He wants me to call." Jesus. So much for her acting ability. She sounded like a nervous wreck. Apparently Luke picked up on it, because warm, steadying hands folded over her shoulders. For a moment, she let herself lean against him. Let his strength support her. Seep into her.

"It will be okay, Trouble. Trust me. Whatever happens, I'm here."

She swallowed the ball of emotion trying to choke her throat, and managed a nod. After hitting the call icon, she wedged the phone to her ear with her shoulder, and reached behind her to tie her bikini top.

Luke's long, nimble fingers took over the task. The second ring ended abruptly as someone picked up on the other end.

"We have a problem." Eddie's no-nonsense voice snapped over the line.

"Callum?" Her pulse raced, thrumming loud in her head. She pressed the phone more tightly to her ear.

"No. I haven't heard from him, and none of the feelers I put out have come back with anything yet. Quinn, this is about you."

Worry for her brother subsided slightly, but a nameless new anxiety licked along her spine. "Me? What have *I* done? I've been here."

"You posed for some pictures. Based on how you look, I'm going to say the photo session occurred about six weeks ago. Needless to say, they were not your best shots."

"I *posed* for pictures? Impossible. I haven't had a shoot since…" Her mind went blank.

"There are four shots—one from every angle. You're wearing underwear."

"Those sound like my—" Her world took a sickening turn, and only the solid feel of Luke at her back stabilized her. "Oh God. I know what they are."

"They hit the tabloids today. All four. Along with some snide speculation about whether the Lena Xavier cat suit comes with Spanx."

"That's impossible." A fog of denial clouded her thoughts, and refused to lift. "I'm the only one who has them." *Except*

Luke. He had them, of course, because he'd taken them, but he wouldn't share them with anyone. "A hack?"

"Doubtful," Eddie said. "We set you up with state-of-the-art security. I wouldn't let any of my clients run around with anything less. Once you've had a high-profile client's personal data compromised, and experienced the joy of FBI agents sniffing around your systems searching for the source of the security breach, you get to be kind of a stickler about stuff like that. But Quinn," he went on, "*how* they leaked is a secondary issue at the moment. What matters is the studio brass panicking. The *Dirty Games* executive producer called me a half-hour ago wanting to cancel your contract. I told her the pictures are old, and you're in the best shape of your life. Then I talked her into meeting with us before she made the stupidest decision of her career."

"When?" She forced the word through numb lips. The cold seeped bone deep. Sharp, icy pain lanced through her chest.

"Tomorrow afternoon, at the studio. Lisa's booking your return flight as we speak. She'll send you the itinerary as soon as it's final."

"Just sent it," his assistant broke in. "You fly out this evening. Everything is taken care of. A car will pick you up from the villa in ninety minutes."

"Okay. All right." An hour and a half to get back to the resort. Clean herself up. Pack. She scrubbed a hand over her face. "I have to get moving."

"Get moving," Eddie agreed. "And Quinn?"

"Yes."

"If you want to keep the role, focus on this. Focus on knocking them on their asses during the meeting tomorrow, because you need to convince them you're the only actress on the planet who can play Lena. I know you're worried about Callum, and you're wondering how the tabloids scored those pictures. I'm on both of those situations. Don't waste time and energy speculating on the what-ifs. I'll update you as soon as I know anything."

"Thanks Eddie. I—" She wanted to tell him there was only one other possible source for the photos, but the words wouldn't come out. "Thank you."

"This is why you pay me fifteen percent. Travel safe, and bring your A game to the meeting." With that, he clicked off the line.

Behind her, Luke's hands stilled. She stepped away from him, and despite the heat of the day, a prickly chill tightened her skin. She dug deep for the nerve to turn and face Luke. He stared at her, eyes intense, his handsome face full of concern.

"What's going on, Trouble?"

"There's a problem." *You were careless, or your security sucks, or…* "I have to go meet with the *Dirty Games* producers pronto and fight for a role I already won once." Her clothes lay in a little pile on the sand where she'd dropped them… what? Twenty minutes ago? Funny how forever could go by so quickly. Trying to keep her mind blank, she picked up her shorts and dragged them on.

"Why?"

"I don't have time to get into it." Frustration sharpened her tone. She turned away and pulled on her shirt before adding, "I have a plane to catch."

"Talk to me, Quinn."

Not a question this time. A command. One she planned to ignore, but when he took hold of her upper arm and tugged her around to face him, she lost her battle for self-control. "The 'Before' pictures you took of me are all over the goddamn internet. The producers are freaking out. They called Eddie to kill my deal. He talked them into meeting with me in person first. But if I don't measure up to their expectations, then…" She couldn't bring herself to finish the sentence.

He simply stared at her for a moment, while the implications seeped in. "Then it's their loss and you'll get another role."

"Yeah, right. I don't know what color the sky is in your world, but in mine, it's not quite so rosy. Word will get out that they fired me because I didn't look the part. My reputation will take a hit. I'll be lucky to land a commercial, much less another movie, and I *need* to work. Callum's rehab doesn't come cheap, and if we ever find him, clearly he's going to have to go back."

He ignored the tirade and focused on the million-dollar question. "Who has access to your digital photos?"

"Nobody. They didn't come from me," she replied. "If you really want the answer to that question, I suspect you'll have to look a little closer to home."

"You think someone got them from me?" He released her and shook his head. "That's impossible."

"Look, you rarely deal with celebrity clients anymore, so cybersecurity probably isn't much of a priority for you. Or maybe someone on your staff decided to make a quick buck?" She shoved her foot into her shoe. "Let's just call it an oversight, unless and until the facts say different."

"No." His voice was soft, but with underlying steel, like freshly poured concrete over rebar. "We secure all our electronics. We have to. We handle peoples' confidential health information and we fully comply with the privacy regulations applicable to that data. Add to that, my staff's ethics are beyond question. Regardless of the conclusions you've drawn about my business, I run a professional operation. Granted, nothing's impenetrable, but in this case, I guarantee nobody hacked your photos from McLean Fitness files, and no member of my team was involved in leaking them."

She shoved her other shoe on, and then braced her hands on her hips. "How can you be so sure?"

He pulled his phone out of the backpack, and then stepped up until they stood toe-to-toe. "Because the photos never went farther than right here." He held up his phone and tapped the screen. "I took the shots, I sent them to you, and then I deleted them. Nothing goes to a cloud. Nothing goes to a storage app. And nobody has access to my texts except me. So you see Quinn, if you're saying the pictures came from my end, what you're really saying is the pictures came from *me*."

A fist of dread gripped her lungs, and made it hard for her to pull in air. She stepped back. "I don't have time to discuss this right now."

He stepped forward. "Do you really think I'd sell you out? Why would I do that?"

A fragment of their conversation from that morning floated through her mind.

I love a grand gesture as much as the next girl, but this has real consequences for you. For your business. Are you sure you know what you're doing?

It will work out. I have a contingency plan.

"You had a contingency plan," she whispered. "Those sites pay good money for really embarrassing celebrity dirt.

His eyes narrowed. "Holy shit, woman. In case you missed it, I just spent five weeks of my life helping you keep this role."

"And then forfeited payment, which put a dent in the books of the important, life-altering business you run." The fist around her chest tightened. "Meanwhile, my career is nothing but a stupid ego jerk-off anyway. I'll get another role, right?"

Dead silence met her question.

"Right. Enough said. Get out of my way, Luke. I have to go." Tears threatened. Where the fuck were her sunglasses?

He crossed his arms, but stood directly in front of her, hemming her in between his body and the bikes. "You're not going anywhere like this. Calm down and tell me what Eddie said."

Ice could burn, she discovered. It could burn white hot. "Calm down? Sure. Let's be calm. Were you calm when you sold me out to some bottom-feeding gossip site? Or did you laugh at what a sad case I was?" She let the sneer stretch her lip. "You bastard. I'll bet you laughed."

More silence met her accusation. The sun picked up the gold in his eyes, and turned it molten. A muscle ticked in his jaw. Finally, he shook his head. "I don't know what you're talking about. All I know for sure is that you owe me an apology."

"Sorry, my mistake. You're not a bastard. I take that back. You're a lying bastard." The insult left a bitter taste on her tongue. She swallowed the venom, and tipped her head back because it was the closest she could come to looking down at him.

He stepped closer and took hold of her chin. "I have never lied to you, Quinn. That's one of the rules, remember?"

His level, unblinking stare almost convinced her. Almost. But by his own admission, there were only two people in the world with access to the photos, and she hadn't sold herself out. "We don't have any rules, *remember*? You canceled our contract."

"Be careful what kind of accusations you fling at me."

Careful wasn't her strong suit. She jerked her chin out of his grasp. "Say you didn't do it. Let's hear it. I dare you."

"If you honestly think I would do that to you, Trouble, there's no point in me wasting my breath. We have nothing left to discuss."

Oh no, he was not going to turn her into the villain. She turned away and spotted her sunglasses in the sand. "You don't give a crap who plays Lena Xavier." She bent to retrieve them. "You consider the whole industry pointless and shallow." Straightening, she slid the glasses over her eyes. "A bunch of bullshit you want no part of."

His expression shuttered, and he took a deliberate step back. Some of her anger fizzled in the face of his withdrawal, and panic ran cold fingers over her skin. *Mission accomplished, Quinn. You've pissed him off.*

"I consider this, right here, a perfect example of the type of bullshit I want no part of."

She turned away and strode to her bike. "Good news, Luke. Me and my bullshit are out of here."

• • •

Luke followed Quinn back to the resort to make sure she didn't end up on the side of the road, and then went back to his room, cracked open a water from the mini-bar while hoping Quinn remembered to hydrate after her ride, and called Eddie. Lisa picked up and put him through.

His friend came on the line with a "Hey, man. Looks like your final week in Paradise will be a vacation."

Yeah, right. He had a business to get back to, and no interest in staying in Paradise Bay without Quinn. He skipped the preliminaries and went straight to the question at hand. "How'd the pictures end up public?"

"I don't know. I'm working on that, but it's going to take some time. Before I get the FBI involved to determine who skimmed whose phone, any chance someone on your team sprung a leak?"

Luke walked out onto his balcony, and sipped the water. "None. I trust my team, but that's irrelevant because I never saved the pictures. The only thing I did was text them to Quinn."

"Maybe someone got them off your phone, directly?"

"No way. Like all my devices, my phone is password protected, and I keep it with me most of the time. Even if someone from housekeeping spent five unattended minutes with it, my phone locks when it's not in use, and nobody has the password except me."

"Hmm."

"Somebody got to them from her end."

"I don't think so. We take measures. I've seen too many celebrities hacked to allow my clients to walk around with their asses hanging out, electronically speaking. She says she didn't share them with anyone."

"She saved them. I told her to, because I wanted her to look at them regularly. Somebody has access to her saved files. A PR person? Whoever updates her social media?"

"No. There's a protocol for that. She would have had to transfer the photos to her publicist. She didn't."

"Somebody's got access," he insisted.

"Apparently," Eddie said. "Look, don't sweat this. It's being handled. My guess is the leak won't be difficult to track down. These web outlets aren't like the Washington Post. They're not especially protective of their sources. I'll have a name within a couple days."

"She thinks I did it."

"What?"

He took another sip of water to wash the bitterness out of his mouth. "You heard me."

"Christ, I *hate* it when my friends start sleeping together. My life is already complicated enough." He expelled a long-suffering sigh. "I'll talk to her."

"Don't bother. I think we covered the relevant facts before she left. I just want to know who's responsible, and make certain she knows."

"Suuuuure that's all you want." He imbued all kinds of

skepticism into the reply. "But before you shove that stick any farther up your ass, keep in mind that she's rattled. Private, unauthorized photos of her are splashed everywhere. Internet trolls are having a field day, and more seriously, the *Dirty Games* producers want to drop her. All she can see right now is that somebody betrayed her, and put something important to her at risk as a result. Maybe cut her some slack and give her a day or two to recover from the shit-storm? Quinn's one of the most loyal people I know, but she isn't used to someone having *her* back."

"*You* have her back," he added.

"I don't count. I'm paid to have her back. And I've known her for a long time. She doesn't have to hide anything from me, because I already know her situation, vis-à-vis Callum."

Her situation. He rolled his shoulders, which did nothing to dislodge the heavy, hollow ache in his chest. "Any word from the brother?"

"Nope. I'm working on that, too."

"He lived with her for how long? Couple months?"

"About five months, I think."

"He bails on rehab, drops out of sight, and less than twenty-four hours later somebody sells private photos of Quinn to a sleazy media outlet. Am I the only one who finds the timing interesting?"

"You're not. But I'm hoping it's just a coincidence because otherwise, it's going to break her heart."

Yeah, he knew how that felt. It fucking sucked.

Chapter Seventeen

"That was fun," Eddie muttered as the elevators doors closed.

Because they had the mirrored and marble vestibule to themselves, Quinn slumped against him and let out the breath she felt as if she'd been holding for the better part of the last twenty-four hours. "Fifteen minutes." She glanced at her watch to confirm that's really all it had been. "Hard to believe the fate of my career came down to a fifteen minute meeting with a room full of suits."

"One you nailed." In the reflection of the doors, she watched his face split into a grin while he loosened his tie. "The executive producer relaxed as soon as you walked into the room. When you took off your jacket, the director's eyes nearly popped out of his head."

She mustered up a weak smile. "That was kind of the point of the outfit." After adjusting the skinny strap of the low-cut, curve-hugging white dress she'd chosen for the meeting, she shrugged on the matching, fitted jacket. There'd been no point in playing coy. Hell, she would have worn the leather cat suit—or nothing at all—if that's what it had taken to secure the role.

"Well, it worked. But you also blew them away with your level of preparation. You delivered a strategic reminder that while they might be able to get another actress who looks the part, nobody else would know the role as well as you. Mentioning how excited you were to work with the director didn't hurt, either."

A discreet *ping* announced their impending arrival at the first floor. A second later, the elevator landed like a cloud and the doors opened with a muted whisper. Eddie stepped aside to let her precede him into the soaring glass box of a lobby.

"If it weren't for the fast talking you did yesterday, I wouldn't have gotten the chance to show them." She stopped and turned to him. "Thanks for working so hard to rescue this deal. I owe you."

He buffed his nails on the lapel of his designer suit. "It would have been their loss."

"Damn right," she agreed, because people expected confidence from her, "but thanks anyway."

Beyond the walls of windows, afternoon sunlight simmered off the Burbank sidewalks. She led them toward the exit while he added, "Are you sure you're cool with doing the interview with *All Access* tomorrow? It would be good to get you in front of cameras sooner rather than later, to counteract the leaked photos. But I can push it back a couple days if you want a little more time before you step into that whirlwind. Once the first interview airs, everybody else is going to line up to talk you."

"Tomorrow's fine. I'm ready to get to work." She slipped dark sunglasses on as she walked through the door he held for her.

"Are you?"

"Of course. Why wouldn't I be?" On the sidewalk, she paused and let the Southern California sun warm her.

She was freezing. The cold that had settled into her bones yesterday evening had turned arctic as she'd sat in the back of an air-conditioned town car on the way to the airport. It had stayed for the flight, through fitful attempts to sleep, and during today's meeting. Part of her was thankful. When the chill finally lifted, this numb sensation insulating her might leave with it. Then she'd really have to *feel*. And while she might have welcomed the heat of anger, or even gnawing worry, she feared what lurked beneath the protective layer of ice was a crushing pain of loss.

"You've taken a couple tough hits in rapid succession. I'm not questioning your professionalism, but I want to be sure you're okay."

"Always." She offered up what felt like a brittle version of the patented Quinn Sheridan smile and brushed nonexistent lint from his shoulder. "Eddie, I'm always okay."

As good an exit line as any. She stepped back, and fought to keep the smile in place. "Later."

He caught her arm, tucked it under his, and steered her across the pavement. "I'll walk you to your car."

"Uh…okay." Her high heels and their height difference required her to take a couple quick steps to match his pace. "Something else on your mind?"

"Yep." He slowed as they approached her SUV. Their reflection appeared in the tinted windshield. "Have you talked to Luke?"

His name had the power to make her miss a step. "No." She looked down and dug through her purse for her key. "I don't plan to. He earned a permanent place on my shit list by selling me out."

"He didn't."

That snapped her attention back to Eddie. "You know who did?"

"Not yet. But I know it wasn't Luke. There has to be

some other explanation."

She found her key and hit the button to unlock the door. "I get that he's your friend and all, but you should know he never denied it."

"He doesn't have to. I *know* he didn't do it. The man is made of ethics. He's also extremely careful. I trust him, and you can, too."

The certainty in his face only made her want to burst into tears. "I don't know if you've noticed this, but I'm not the kind of girl who inspires a hell of a lot of caring from anyone."

"That's not true. You've got a family fairly inept at demonstrating it, but you can't take their shortcomings and project them onto the rest of the world. You're not being fair to yourself, or Luke."

"It doesn't matter." She started to shake as the truth of those words sank in—little shivers that, ironically, signaled the melting away of her icy fortitude. Before she fell apart in a studio parking lot, she wrenched open the car door and climbed behind the wheel.

"Quinn—"

"It doesn't matter," she repeated, cutting him off. "If I'm right, Luke fucked me. If you're right…" She broke off to absorb the stunningly sharp stab of pain. "If you're right, I fucked myself, because he'll never speak to me again."

• • •

Good news never came at two in the morning. Quinn had known as much before she'd picked up the phone, but walking into a police station an hour later only confirmed it. She posted bail on Callum's behalf, and then waited another hour, all the while thanking God she was sitting in a police station instead of a hospital or a morgue. Eventually an officer brought her brother out, looking pale and hollow eyed under the harsh fluorescent lights.

They both held it together until they were ensconced in the privacy of her SUV. As soon as he shut his door, she turned to him, and even though she'd spent the wait time coaching herself to stay calm, the emotional rollercoaster she'd been on for too long simply bottomed out. She smacked his shoulder, and yelled, "So help me God, Callum…"

"I know. Jesus. *Ow!* Quinn, I'm sorry. I screwed up. I am so…fucking…sorry." Then he buried his face in his hands—hands so grimy, even the gloomy interior of the car couldn't hide the dirt—and for one hysterical second, she wondered just how they fingerprinted people nowadays. Then he broke down in silent, body-wracking sobs.

She'd wanted to see remorse from him. Wanted actual tears, and uncontrolled sobs as evidence he knew what he'd put her through with his choices—what he'd put the whole family through. But now that he was sitting in her passenger seat all wrung out and shattered, she couldn't help gathering him up. He was her brother. Her twin. They'd never existed independent of each other. Their mom had a grainy gray-and-white ultrasound image of them snuggled up together in the womb and whatever link had been forged way back then still tethered them, despite the way their paths had diverged. She never planned to cut that tie.

"It's okay." She tightened her arms around him, and pulled him close, startled at how much it felt like hugging a bag of bones, despite the oversize black hoodie he wore. He buried his face against her shoulder, and cried out a torrent of guilt, fear, embarrassment, self-pity, and maybe…hopefully, some relief. Hot, wet tears soaked through the gray cardigan she'd thrown over her T-shirt and cut-offs. "It's going to be okay," she whispered again, and kissed the top of his head. "Let's get out of here."

"Uh-uh." He drew away, but didn't look at her. "It's not

okay, and we shouldn't go anywhere yet. You don't know. I did something bad, Quinnie." He sniffed and wiped his eyes, focused them on some point beyond the windshield. "A real doucher move."

Mostly to assure him nothing would shock her, she said, "Did you lie? Did you steal? Callum Sheridan, did you sell your body for drugs?"

"No." His denial was quiet. Ominous. His eyes darted to hers, and then away. "I sold yours."

Now it was her turn to draw back. "You did…what?"

"When I left Foundations, I hooked up with Damon and Bhodi. Remember them?"

Vaguely. Bhodi was another actor who'd aged out of the spotlight in his teens. Damon, as far as she could tell, was a periodic drug dealer and full-time fuckup. She nodded.

"We partied for a while, but then we needed money to keep the party going. I might have been throwing your name around to look like hot shit—I probably was. Anyway, Damon ran into this friend who had a friend who works for some Gawker-type site, and she had big brown eyes and a baggie of coke, and kept talking about how maybe we could work something out if I could give her an inside track, and I kind of…" He looked away again and squinted out the windshield into the darkness.

"You kind of did what, Callum?" But her heart crashed into her ribs because she already knew.

"I kind of said that I thought I could guess your cloud password—just FYI you need to pick a better one than last name and our birthday—and then next thing I knew, we had more shit, and pictures of you in your underwear were all over the internet. I'm really sorry, Quinn," he went on quickly. "I understand if you want to walk back into the police station and press charges for identity theft, or hacking or whatever. I don't care. I have it coming. I'll do whatever it takes to make you forgive me."

A landslide of thoughts tumbled through her mind. She gripped the steering wheel to get her bearings, but slowing the rush long enough to pick a sensible reaction out of the torrent felt next to impossible. "I'm not going to press charges against you, Callum. You're my brother, for Christ's sake, and you have a problem. But I can't continue being collateral damage to your recklessness. That can't happen anymore. "

"I know."

She barely heard him. "I have to protect myself. I can't trust you."

"I'll change. I swear. I'll win your trust back."

"You..." Luke's voice replayed in her head, and shaped her reply. "You have to *earn* it. You have to go back to Foundations, and you have to finish this time. That's step one."

"I know," he repeated, sounding miserable but strangely resigned. "I can't do this anymore, either. I can't stand myself, Quinnie. I can't stand that I hurt you. Again."

Hurt her? Hurt seemed like an insufficient description of the state she was in. Emotions churned to the surface. "I blamed someone else. Someone important to me." Tears scalded her cheeks. "I called him a bastard to his face and pushed him away."

"I'll talk to him—"

"No!" She took a deep breath, and tried to clear an image of that disaster from her mind. She really would be picking her brother up at the morgue if she let Luke get within striking distance of Callum. "No. This isn't something you can fix."

"This is the guy you were cozy with on Paradise Bay?"

Exhaling helped her release her death grip on the steering wheel. "It wasn't like that. He came as a favor to Eddie—to help me salvage my shot at *Dirty Games*. But for Eddie cashing in a chip, he would have chosen to have nothing to do with me."

"Then he's an asshole, Quinnie. I'm not saying that to justify my fucking things up for you, but any guy who doesn't thank his lucky stars to be near you doesn't deserve your time. You're smart, fun, and you're determined. People like Eddie call in favors for you for a reason. You're the real deal, Quinn. I mean it. You have your shit together. Even when we were small, and I was the star and you were Callum Sheridan's sister, I knew there was something inside you—some core of strength. Hell, I don't know how to explain it. It's something I didn't have."

"My shit is together?" She almost laughed at how off the mark her brother was, but, then again, he spoke from the perspective of a guy who'd just walked out of a jail cell. "Not really. Luke knows better. He saw the absolute worst of me—an ungrateful, argumentative woman with a self-defeating streak a mile wide, hiding her insecurity behind pride and a fuck-you smile. For some reason he stuck by me anyway. He pushed past all my defenses, and actually gave a damn about *me*. And I paid him back by calling him a lying bastard and accusing him of betraying me. No explanation I offer can undo that." She swallowed the truth like a bitter pill. "There is no fixing this."

The weight of that was too much to bear. She rested her aching head against the seatback and let the stinging tears flow from beneath her closed eyes.

Something soft touched her face, disappeared, and then returned with more insistence. Belatedly, she realized Callum was wiping tears from her cheek with the sleeve of his sweatshirt.

The little-boy sweetness of the gesture threatened to shatter what was left of the heart she'd broken to pieces all on her own. She ducked away. "Jesus, don't even. Where has that thing been?"

The snide comment earned her a sheepish laugh. "I'm pretty sure it's yours," he confessed, and continued drying her tears. "I borrowed it when I was living with you. Sorry. I'll get you a new one."

It was just pathetic enough to wring a laugh out of her. A tired one, but still. She opened her eyes and looked at him. "In the grand scheme of things, I'm not too concerned about replacing a sweatshirt."

He gave her a patient, almost wise smile. "It's not really about replacing the sweatshirt, it's about making amends—acknowledging the harm and restoring justice as much as possible."

She sniffed, and then gave up and wiped her face with her own sleeve. "Making amends, huh?"

"Yep. We learn about it in recovery. Some mistakes can't be undone, but you can always make amends in some way. It's how you fix things."

"You think?"

"Mmm-hmm," he replied in his version of Yoda's simultaneously guttural and sing-song-y voice, and poked her in the shoulder. "Fix things, you must."

Chapter Eighteen

Luke approached a treadmill where a bearded, tattooed lumberjack of a guy sweated through a warm-up. Six months ago, the warehouse manager and one-time high school wrestling champ wouldn't have survived the first mile. At intake, he'd been sixty pounds overweight, recovering from a heart attack, and afraid of leaving his wife a widow before he'd seen any of their four kids graduate from kindergarten. Today, thirty-five pounds lighter and far more active, Luke noted with satisfaction Dale Metcalf jogged comfortably at a ten-minute-mile pace.

Apparently sensing an audience, the man's attention wandered from the news program playing on the flat screen mounted in front of the line of treadmills to the mirrored wall where both their forms were reflected. Teeth flashed beneath the Grizzly Adams beard. "Ah, Christ, McLean, you've gotten even uglier since I last saw you."

"I missed you, too, Dale." He did his best to muster up a kiss-my-ass sneer, but it felt flat. Flying back from Paradise Bay alone with a hole in his chest where his heart should have been had effectively sucked whatever was left of his sense of humor away. Three days back in his normal routine had done little to restore it. He missed her, dammit. Worse, he was about one more miserable, lonesome night away from doing something pathetic like calling Eddie and asking him if Quinn had mentioned him.

Dark eyes assessed him in the mirror and the grin disappeared. "You know, you look kind of bleak for a guy who just got back from a long vacation at a swanky resort."

"Wasn't a vacation. I went there for work."

"Poor you. My work never takes me to an island in the Carib-fucking-bean." The eyes narrowed. "And yet, you're wound tighter than my mother-in-law at Thanksgiving dinner. Is it possible you went to a tropical paradise and somehow managed to not get laid? That's gotta suck. No wonder you're all tense and shit."

"I'm not tense. If you want to worry about something"—out of habit, he checked the heart rate monitor readout and noted it was in a good range—"worry about your own sex life."

Dale laughed. "Are you kidding? The wife can't keep her hands off me, and since I've dropped some weight, we can get up into some damn interesting…ah…positions. She likes this one—I call it the naked skiing accident—where she goes low"—he dropped his hand to demonstrate— "and I go high, and she does this thing with her leg—"

"Consult your doctor to confirm you're healthy enough for sex."

"Consult this." He flipped Luke the bird. "If I can survive running three miles a day, every damn day, I can fuck my wife standing up. The heart doc gave me the okay months ago. The only thing I have to worry about is baby number five, which is going to happen sooner rather than later if we don't watch it."

"There are plenty of reliable ways of avoiding surprises, you know."

"Not when you marry a good Catholic girl. Just gotta watch the calendar and plan accordingly."

"Good luck with that." Because he noticed the news had transitioned to an ad for a pregnancy test, he took the remote from the holder on the treadmill and punched up the volume.

"*Ha.* Good to see your raging case of blue balls hasn't affected your smart ass. Find me some sports or something. I don't mind putting in two more miles, but I'd rather not be there for them, if you know what I mean."

Obliging, Luke flipped through the channels.

"Wait. Back one."

He tuned the TV to the channel Dale requested, and adjusted the volume. "*All Access*? Seriously?"

Dale shrugged as best he could midstride. "My wife loves this show. She got me hooked. Besides, where else am I going to see something like *that,* without ending up in divorce court?"

Luke froze. The camera was doing a slow pan up long, lean legs clad in tight, black leather. The shot continued up toned thighs, slender, curving hips, a narrow waist, high, round, painfully familiar breasts cupped faithfully by supple leather, and cleavage displayed to perfection thanks to a zipper that hadn't found its way north of her navel.

His gut clenched, even before the camera continued its slow journey to her face. Then his heart tripped, because Quinn Sheridan stood there, framed in the lens. Her blond hair was now a disorienting, inky black, which made her look exotic and dangerous, but her lips curved into the daredevil smile still haunting his dreams.

"She is fuckhot," Dale whispered, almost reverently.

Luke ignored that, and punched up the volume because one of the "reporters" on the show—an avid-eyed brunette with over-styled hair and a big, shark-like smile—stepped up with a microphone and asked Quinn a question.

"Thanks, Nancy," she said, apparently responding to a comment from the reporter. Her voice sounded almost the same. Almost as smooth and nuanced as in real life. She ran a hand over her hip. "I worked really hard to get into shape for this bad boy." Then she gave her ass a smack.

"You've definitely succeeded," the interviewer gushed.

"I didn't do it alone," Quinn added. "Or gracefully, to be honest. I was coming off an injury, I hadn't worked out in months, and I was feeling a little panicked at the prospect of slipping into this costume in a few weeks. So I went to this beautiful resort called Paradise Bay, and worked with a guy named Luke McLean who was amazing. Just amazing."

"Holy shit," Dale murmured. "You've met her. You've touched her. You're single. She's single. Please tell me you—"

"I'm not telling you anything, other than to shut up so I can listen." He bumped the volume another notch.

"...designed a safe, healthy plan for turning me from a couch potato to badass Lena Xavier in less than six weeks," Quinn said. "He cleaned up my diet, revved my metabolism, reacquainted me with the strong, resilient body I'd taken for granted too long, and maybe most importantly, he called me out on some bad habits I'd developed that undermined my goals."

"You look amazing," Nancy replied with over-the-top enthusiasm. "Sounds like more than just a six-week boot camp in preparation for a role."

"So much more." Quinn looked straight at the camera. "He didn't just change my body. He changed *me*. I didn't properly appreciate everything he did—and how completely in my corner he was—until recently. I definitely owe him... so much."

Was there a message in there, or was he hearing what he

wanted to hear?

"I've seen the 'Before' pictures someone leaked—"

Quinn rolled her eyes and let out a little laugh. "Nancy, I feel like the entire world has seen the 'Before' pictures. I never dreamed there would be such an audience for shots of me standing around in my underwear. Now that I know, I'm bummed I had to leave before I could take the 'After' pictures. I want someone to leak those!"

"I understand the studio executives were concerned, to say the least, when those 'Before' shots surfaced. They considered going with another actress."

"I honestly don't know if they considered other actresses for the role. I can only say I'm excited to be their final choice and..." She struck a hip-jutting, laser-eyed pose at the camera. "What do you think, people? Am I ready for my 'After' pictures?"

The reporter laughed. "I think our Twitter feed is about to explode. I vote yes."

Quinn looked into the camera again, her expression utterly serious. "Hey, Luke, if you're watching, come get your 'After' shots. Anytime. I'm prepared to bare it all to you."

Nancy aimed a conspiratorial look at the screen. "This time *All Access* gets the exclusive first peek."

The program flicked over to a commercial. Luke stared unseeingly at the screen and rubbed his chest where a dull ache throbbed just from watching her, listening to her, in a stupid three-minute interview.

"Are you still here?" Dale's voice broke into his haze of yearning. Then a big, meaty fist hit him in the shoulder. "What the fuck, man? That goddess just offered to get naked for you."

She'd offered a whole lot more, he hoped, because he wasn't going to settle for anything less than everything.

• • •

Quinn swung through the door to her trailer, barely waiting for the slam of metal against metal before her fingers felt for the zipper to the cat suit. An afternoon of standing, running, crouching, leaping, and rolling in front of a green screen for the technical team verified one important fact. Leather didn't breathe. She tipped her head to work a kink out of her neck, and then stopped, zipper halfway to her crotch, when she realized she wasn't alone.

"Luke?" She stood stock-still, but inside, her system raced in reaction to seeing him there. She tried to drink in every part of him at once, as he sat with loose-limbed grace on the small sofa in the cramped space. His sun-burnished hair tempted her fingers. His intent eyes sent nervous energy licking along her skin. His white button-down shirt stretched across shoulders she knew firsthand were strong enough to hold her while he used his mouth to send her to heaven.

"Hello, Trouble. Eddie let me in. Hope you don't mind."

"No." Despite feeling dizzy, she shook her head, and then stepped a little closer and looked around the trailer.

"He's not here. It's just me. We're alone."

"Oh." *'Oh'? For days you've been rehearsing what you would say to the man if he ever spoke to you again, and 'Oh' is the best you can do?*

"Does that door have a lock?"

"Huh?" *Holy shit, Quinn, stop with the flowery speeches.* "I…yes."

"Lock it."

She did as he asked, and then turned back to him.

"Your fingers are shaking. Are you nervous?"

He'd noticed that small detail from all the way over there. He missed nothing. "No. I'm not nervous."

She was a nervous wreck. She wanted to see him. She'd

hoped he'd come. But now that he was here, all her carefully thought-out explanations and apologies fled, and left her with nothing except…want. Need. Love. What if she just threw herself at his feet, and begged him to give her another chance? "You surprised me. That's all."

"I caught your interview on that show. I came to take you up on your offer."

"'After' shots?"

He nodded. "Yep."

"Now?"

"You said anytime. Strip, Trouble. Down to your underwear." He sat back, and crossed his arms. "Or don't you trust me?"

"I trust you, Luke. I do." Her hand hovered on the zipper. "There's only one little problem…"

The way his eyes heated when she said she trusted him eased her nerves. Now her hands shook for other reasons.

"As long as you trust me, we've got no problems."

"Okaaaay." She toed off one of the spike-heeled leather booties, the other, and then slowly lowered the zipper that ran down the front of the costume. It took another couple seconds to peel her arms out of the sleeves, and another still to ease her hands under the leather and prepare to slide it down her hips.

"Christ, Quinn, are you—"

"Uh-huh." She pushed the outfit down to her knees, and undid the zippers running along the outsides of her ankles. "That's the problem. I'm not wearing any underwear." She freed her legs, one at a time, and stepped out of the suit. Slowly, she straightened. "Nothing to ruin the lines of the costume."

He just stared at her.

The nerves came back with a vengeance. "There's this, like, nylon body-stocking layer inside, so it's not as uncomfortable as it sounds. Do you have your phone, or a camera, or…" Shit, she was babbling. She was naked, and babbling, and… "I'm so sorry." Crying. "I'm sorry I accused you of selling me out. P-please forgive me, Luke." Good lord. Not just crying. Ugly crying. She turned away and tried to get herself together.

Big hands closed on her shoulders and eased her back against a warm, solid wall of man. "You're forgiven, under one condition."

"Anything." She drew in a deep breath, as strong arms enfolded her. "Any condition. Any consequence, or punishment. Name it. I know I deserve it."

His low laugh fanned her neck. "Don't give me any ideas, Trouble. The condition is that you forgive me, too."

Confusion had her turning in his arms. "Forgive you? For what?"

"For allowing you to believe I lacked respect for your career."

"It's okay—"

"It's not okay." He tightened his hold on her, and rested his forehead against hers. "I disparaged something important to you. Even at the beginning, before I knew you, I realized your career meant a lot to you. At best, I treated it like a frivolous pursuit, and at worst, called it bullshit. What I should have said, weeks ago, was that I admire you for knowing what you're passionate about, and following that passion. What I should have said, Quinn, is that I love you, and I want to support you in whatever fulfills you. Will you trust me to do better with that in the future?"

"I do. Trust me, too, Luke." She pressed a hand to his cheek. "I want to give you the same. I know we met because I needed you to drop everything going on in your life and attend to me, but I swear I'm not that girl."

"I know." He cupped her jaw in his hands and kissed her

long, and deep. So long and deep, she was battling tears again when he raised his head. But this time they were joyful tears. Still, she blinked them away, fished his phone from his jeans pocket, and stepped out of his arms.

"Trouble?"

She handed him the phone, and then pushed her shoulders back and shook her hair out. "I believe we have some 'After' shots to take."

"We don't have to. You don't have to prove anything to me. I know you know I didn't sell the others."

"*I* want you to have them." Lifting her chin, she sent him a silent challenge. "I'm not the same woman I was six weeks ago. It's got nothing to do with a flat stomach, or a toned ass. It's not because of any physical transformation. It's because I'm in love with you, Luke McLean. That's the 'After' and I want *you* to see. So take your damn pictures."

He tossed the phone over his shoulder, and gathered her into his arms again. "I don't need a picture. I only need you." Then he lowered his mouth to hers and proved it—until her legs clamped around his waist, his hands gripped her hips, and they both struggled for air.

She stared into his eyes and rocked herself against his hard-on. "I think some parts of you are definitely in need."

He scowled at her from under his brows. "That's a consequence of you prancing around naked."

Laughter bubbled in her throat. "You know, I'm a big believer in consequences."

"That's good, because I've got a big consequence and it's all for you."

"Is that a threat, Mr. McLean?"

"That's a promise, Trouble. Forever."

Acknowledgments

Massive thanks to Cathryn Fox for conceiving of this series, inviting me to go to Paradise Bay, and to Suzanne Rock and Daire St. Dennis for joining the fun and games. Get it? *Games?!*

Equally massive thanks to the readers, particularly those of you who caught the *Dirty Games* teasers I posted on my Facebook author page and/or in the Racy Reads Party Room, and responded with hearts, stickers, and "Fanning my vagina" gifs. There are simply no words to describe what that sort of encouragement does for me.

An inappropriately long hug to Brenda Chin, for green-lighting this project. It took years of scheming on my part, but I finally got to work with you. I feel so legit!

Unending gratitude to Liz, Curtis, Heather, Melanie, Jessica, Riki, Kari, and the rest of the Entangled team for all your expertise.

Sloppy kisses to Robin Bielman and Hayson Manning for the writing dates, drinks, beach breaks, drinks, lunches, drinks, dinners, drinks…

Love, love, love to my family and friends. I'm the lucky one. You know it. More importantly, I know it.

About the Author

Wine lover, sleep fanatic, and *USA Today* Bestselling Author of sexy contemporary romance novels, Samanthe Beck lives in Malibu, California, with her long-suffering but extremely adorable husband and their turbo-son. Throw in a furry ninja named Kitty and Bebe the trash talking Chihuahua and you get the whole, chaotic picture.

When not dreaming up fun, fan-your-cheeks sexy ways to get her characters to happily-ever-after, she searches for the perfect cabernet to pair with Ambien.

CPSIA information can be obtained
at www.ICGtesting.com
Printed in the USA
LVHW112334031022
729892LV00019B/222